CW00382398

TABLE OF CONTENTS

ABOUT THIS BOOK

Vacationing can be troublesome. Will Pauline and Nona solve the mysteries before they become victims?

Seeking friendly companionship and a bit of solace from their sleuthing days gone by, Pauline and Nona adventure together on six whirlwind vacations in the United States and Canada, that are anything but relaxing. Travel forward from the Miss Riddell series to the twenty-first century with the demure Miss Pauline Riddell and her fly-by-the-seat of her pants cohort, Nona.

These stories can be read in any order.
The last story ends on a cliffhanger.

Move forward twenty years from the Miss Riddell Series by P.C. James and backward in time twenty years from Sewing Suspicion Quilting Cozy Mysteries by Kathryn Mykel—setting these stories to be after the turn of the 21st century, between 2004-2010.

Join us in the Adventures of Pauline and Nona Facebook group:

From the creative writers: P.C. James, author of the Best-Selling Miss Riddell Cozy Mystery Series and Kathryn Mykel, Award-Winning author of Best-Selling Sewing Suspicion, Quilting Cozy Mystery.

SASSY SENIOR SLEUTHS MYSTERIES

7

MURDER AT SEA

P.C. JAMES
KATHRYN MYKEL

MURDER AT SEA

Mini Mystery #7

Pauline and her friend Nona lay on the cruise ship *Adonia's* loungers, gazing up at the starlit sky, when Nona said, "I'm glad we skipped the show tonight." The two long-time sleuthing partners were once again on vacation together, this time on a Caribbean cruise.

Pauline nodded and sighed. "This is nature at its best. I think I could count every star, they're so bright now that the sun's gone down."

"What time is the red-*Blood Moon* supposed to start?" Nona asked.

"Around nine, so we've a few hours to wait."

"We'll need warmer clothes by then," Nona said. "It's already growing chilly."

Rubbing her shoulders, Pauline commented, "That sunburn of yours won't help any. I can't believe it's ever cold in the

Caribbean. Seven days of glorious heat is a welcome escape from the icy temps in Toronto."

"And snow, in Massachusetts," Nona replied. "The lights of Jamaica are almost out of sight." She pointed towards the horizon beyond the stern.

"A beautiful island, but I'm pleased to be away from everybody now, watching the heavens put on a show for us." A shooting star flashed across the sky.

"I enjoyed climbing Dunn's Falls," Nona reminisced. "Though I think some of our fellow passengers became overly excited about mountaineering beyond their capabilities."

Pauline smiled. "Like that crazy old man trying to shimmy up the palm tree when on the beach."

"Exactly like that. He was lucky he wasn't hurt."

"The soft sand took all the force of the thump when he landed," Pauline added, laughing to herself.

"Sure, but I imagine he'll have a bruised heinie for weeks," Nona said, giggling. "Serves him right."

"You're right, though," Pauline added. "It did get a lot of people excited. You wouldn't expect that behavior out of such an old crowd."

"Will men ever truly believe they're not still nineteen and able to conquer the world?"

"Just big kids at heart, right to the end—some of them," Pauline murmured.

The two women lounged in silence for a few minutes, then Nona sat up. "I'm going to get a jacket . . . and a blanket. Do you want one?" She rubbed the chill from her arms.

"Yes, please." Pauline was about to get up when a sickening thump nearby made her scramble to her feet.

"What was that?" Nona asked, her head swiveling around.

"I hope it wasn't what I think it was," Pauline replied.

"A *really* foolish man?" Nona mumbled and jumped up from

her lounger. "Oh, I shouldn't have done that! Vertigo." Nona set out a hand to steady herself.

Pauline hurried along the deck towards the bow of the ship, in the direction of the thudding.

"No, really, don't worry about me, I'll catch up," Nona called out behind her.

Turning a corner, the amateur sleuth came upon a body, lying crumpled on the deck. No other passengers were anywhere in sight. Nona arrived a moment later. "I think the vertigo has passed now. Him too, from the looks of it."

Pauline bent and grasped the man's wrist, while Nona bent and placed her fingertips on his throat. This wasn't the first body they'd witnessed and likely wouldn't be the last. The two waited for signs of life and then they both shook their heads.

"As I suspected, he's dead," Nona concluded. "I know I should be surprised by that fact—."

"I think I remember him from our tour today. Our prediction looks to have come to fruition."

"Wasn't this the man climbing the palm tree earlier?" Nona pulled out a handkerchief and dabbed sweat from her forehead. "Maybe he was climbing something on the deck above and slipped?" Nona looked up. The decks above were void of life too.

"Regardless, we should remain calm," Pauline stated.

"Since when have we not been calm in the face of a murder mystery."

"You're getting ahead of yourself, Nona. A simple case of 'slip and fall.'"

"Now who's getting ahead of themselves," Nona scoffed.

Pauline darted her eyes around. "We need to find an emergency button. Do you remember seeing one nearby?"

"Yes, just around the corner. I'm always on alert for panic buttons, emergency exits and unusual weapons." Nona grinned. "I'll go." Her sandals clacked rapidly against the deck and her straight platinum blonde hair bobbed in the wind as she scurried off.

Moments later the ship's alarm blared and flashing lights shot across the darkening sky and unusually empty deck. Pauline recoiled and then covered her ears. Gawkers arrived one after another until there was a crowd huddled around the body. Pauline held them back with outstretched arms. She breathed a sigh of relief when Nona finally emerged from around the corner with the ship's security right behind her.

The sirens ceased and Nona jammed a finger in her ear. "Between the vertigo and the eardrum-blowing screeching I can't walk straight."

Pauline pulled on her arm. "Security can handle the matter from here, we don't want to get involved."

"What?" Nona yelled.

"I said... Oh, never mind."

"Yes, I agree we should offer our services."

"I said, we should *not* get involved," Pauline urged.

"I agree. I'm sure they're going to want to question us, let's stick around a bit," Nona replied.

A young woman, all business, approached, her *Adonia* security badge displayed her name as Rita. "What's happened here?"

Nona shrugged and yelled. "We only heard the thud."

"We don't have anything to add," Pauline said, in a hushed tone and Nona gave her a puzzled look.

"If hearing his body land is all you know," Rita said, "we won't be but a minute taking your statements, and you can enjoy the rest of the evening without further interruption."

Pauline pulled Nona away from the scene as the security personnel cleared the crowd. "I don't want to get involved in this one," Pauline whispered. "I had a case like this years ago, and the mystery spoiled the cruise for me."

"What? I can't hear a thing," Nona said, poking her finger in her ear one more time as if the ringing would magically go away.

"Will you stop with that already?"

More ship's crew arrived to clear the scene and take the body away. Pauline inserted herself in between the crew and the dead man. "Wait. You need to at least photograph the scene for clues."

"Madam, please step aside," Rita replied. "We have accidents on ships all the time. While they're terribly sad, they are hardly police matters. We have procedures and we'll follow them carefully, you can be sure. Please follow my associate here into the lounge, and we'll take your statements." Her black and gold uniform added additional support to her authority.

"He could've slipped and fallen from the balconies above," Nona said, pointing upward.

"People climb and sit on the railings all the time," Rita replied. "Did you see anyone at the balconies above when you found the body?"

"No," Nona and Pauline replied in unison.

"Well then," Rita replied. "As I said, an unfortunate accident. They don't happen often, but when they do it's often to men like him."

"You know him?" Pauline asked.

Rita shrugged. "I know *of* him and his recent…"

"Oh, you're aware of the climbing incident," Nona interjected.

Rita nodded.

Two staff members carried the body away on a stretcher. Pauline shook her head as they passed her, frowning at the disturbingly gloating smiles on their faces.

"Did you see the expressions of those stretcher-bearers?" She asked Nona as they too walked away from the accident site.

"Either they see 'accidents' as often as we do or they were just grimacing at the weight," Nona replied.

"Looked like they were gloating," Pauline replied. "How odd. As if they were pleased about something. Maybe happy that we confirmed there was no one on the balconies above. That's my theory." Pauline paused. "What's your gut telling you?"

"That it's weird they just carted off the body like that? Where will they put it? Ice cream freezer?" Nona asked.

"No, they will have a shipboard morgue."

"Now that's intriguing. We still have no evidence of any wrongdoing, Pauline. Could be just a drunk man acting stupidly," Nona suggested. "I thought you didn't want to be involved in this one?"

Pauline smiled sheepishly.

"Let's get a drink." Nona pointed to the *Mojito Tank* across the deck where a bartender was wiping down the wooden plank that served as the bar.

"I don't think that was open earlier," Pauline observed.

"It's like they opened it just for the crowd." Nona waved her hand to the dispersing people heading straight for the bar and laughed. "Capitalism."

Pauline knitted her brows. "What did you make of Rita's answer when you asked if she knew the victim?"

"I didn't think anything of it." Nona shrugged. "I asked, she shrugged then nodded. What else was there about that? I'm more inclined to suspect the other staffers."

"We'd better not get drinks just yet." Pauline turned. "Let's just give our statements, before they think it was us who did him in."

"The deck did him in, Pauline. We had nothing to do with it."

When they gave their statements, the details were as bare as the sunbathers that they'd seen on the islands they'd visited. There was nothing to say other than they'd heard the thud of the body hitting the deck.

THE NEXT DAY, Pauline was reading under an awning on the shaded side of the ship. Nona bustled over to her with two frozen concoctions. Each with a skewer of fresh fruit and a little plastic monkey hanging over the edge of the glass.

"What do you think, Pauline?" Nona said, spilling some of the ice-cold drink on Pauline's bare leg as she placed the glasses on the table between their loungers.

"Freezing, is what I think," Pauline said, wiping her thigh with her hand. "Whatever I suspect, I didn't need to be wet to think it."

"Don't be stiff, Pauline." Nona plunked herself into the other chair. "That man's fall was surely not an accident."

Pauline groaned. "So you still want to investigate?"

"Yup, and so do you. I know you too well. You've been gazing out to sea all morning in that curious way you have when you're puzzling over the details of a case."

Pauline ignored the aspersion on her thoughtful expression. "What do we know that points to anything other than an accident?"

"That's a silly question. In all the years we've had bodies landing in our laps, so to speak, it's never once been an *accident*. Besides, the rumor is: he was dead before the fall and"—Nona paused for dramatic effect—"he's not just a tourist. He is, well he was, a government agent."

"An agent, Nona? Where did you hear this? Is this just another one of your wild theories? One of these days I'm going to start asking questions about what you really do when we're not on vacation," Pauline jested and eyed the frozen drinks.

Nona zipped her lips in a mocking gesture before sucking on the rainbow colored straw in the drink cup.

Pauline shook her head. "Do you mean like a clerk in the driving-license bureau?"

Nona erupted in a hyena-like laugh, and Pauline waited for her to cease her antics before asking, "Who told you he was a government agent?"

"His wife. She's telling anyone who will listen." Nona slurped her drink and winced. "Argh, brain freeze!"

"Sunburn, vertigo, now brain freeze...what's next?" Pauline asked.

Nona licked her lips. Her tongue was purple. "She said she thought there was someone on the cruise out to get her husband."

Pauline rubbed the glossy cover of her new book. "I suppose we should talk to the wife before the cruise people silence her."

"Taken care of," Nona said. "She was at the bar. I told her that we are super sleuths and agreed to meet her at lunch today, in the *Spanish Grill*."

Pauline checked her watch. "I assume you also made a reservation?"

"Not yet," Nona said. "We can do it now." She rolled up and out of the lounge chair.

They made their way to the specialty restaurant and arranged the reservation for the meeting. Leaving the restaurant, Nona pointed to a middle-aged man hobbling along the side of the indoor pool. "Hey, isn't he the one who fell from the tree?"

Pauline studied the man, and the baseball-sized, black and blue blotch that showed just above his swim trunks. "I think it is, but . . ."

"He looks a bit like the dead man," Nona said in a questioning tone.

Pauline nodded. "I think we confused the two men. The victim wasn't the one who fell from the tree." They plopped down in two seats under an umbrella. "Other than confirming that for us, do you think the widow will have anything useful to say?"

"Even if she doesn't, it's better than sitting here watching the waves go by," Nona muttered.

"Are you becoming sea sick?"

"No, but I'd rather not add that to my list, too," Nona replied.

"We were perfectly content with the waves *before* there was a case to investigate."

"Sure, sure."

"Okay then, let's start by visiting the scene of the crime," Pauline suggested, "or at least where he landed and where he might have fallen from."

"According to gossip, he didn't fall; he was thrown over," Nona said, as they made their way to the part of the deck blocked off with rope serving as a crime scene barrier.

"Since when do we investigate cases based on gossip?" Pauline asked, standing at the rope and gazing up at the many decks above.

Nona ducked under the barrier while Pauline continued, "The trouble is, he probably came down from one of those balconies, and we'll never get into the suites to investigate."

"Unless one of them is *his* suite," Nona said. "After all, the most likely suspect is his wife. We should find out if he was killed first and then pushed over."

"I agree," Pauline said. "Pretending there's a killer on board would be the perfect way to cover her tracks."

"The deck above is available to everyone. Let's start there."

As they rounded the top of the outdoor steps, this deck was roped off also. Peering around, there were no clues in sight to suggest anyone had ever been here, let alone to suggest a struggle between a killer and his or her victim.

"If this is the scene of the crime," Nona said, "we can rule out the wife. She's too small. I doubt she weighs 110 pounds, and he was twice that, at least. She couldn't carry his body here and throw that weight over without help."

Pauline stared at the balconies above. "The same is true of those higher balconies. No one could have thrown his body over with the way they're arranged, each one set back from the one below as they get closer to the top." She shaded her eyes with her hand; the sun was high overhead. "The killer would have to throw the body out a long way, or it would just land on the balcony below. It's really just those first two that are possibilities, looking at them from here."

"Agreed," Nona said. "If the dead man's cabin is either of those two suites, his wife could be the culprit. If not, it's a mystery man."

As they arrived at the *Spanish Grill*, the widow was drowning her sorrows. Empty shot glasses littered the table. The two sleuths exchanged glances as the woman wobbled in her seat across the room. They approached the wife's table and sat quickly. Madelyn looked up and let out a loud belch before covering her face with a menu.

"As I told you previously, Madelyn," Nona said, "Pauline and I have solved lots of cases the police couldn't and we'd like to help you."

Madelyn nodded, but her attention was distracted by her empty glass. She ran her finger around the lip of the cup.

"Do you understand what she's saying?" Pauline asked, as the woman raised her hand to flag the waiter.

"Madelyn, maybe you could start by telling us where your cabin is?" Nona asked.

"Right above . . . above where he landed," Madelyn slurred,

and then burped again. She raised her hand again with her empty glass in hand this time.

"He probably fell from your balcony, then," Pauline said.

Madelyn giggled. "I can understand why you're such a hotshot detective."

"Were you there when he fell?" Nona asked.

Madelyn blinked as if she'd just noticed her companions. "Obviously not."

"Was someone in your room with your husband?"

Madelyn shook her head. "I told all this to that security woman."

"Was your husband meeting someone?" Pauline asked. "Were you aware he was in the cabin?"

Madelyn's head bobbed; the color in her face was fading. "I must go . . ." she gasped, struggling off her chair, causing the seat to fall over before she hurried in the direction of the washrooms.

The waiter dropped off her drink and turned the chair right side up.

"It's her," Nona said. "I don't believe a word of her not knowing her husband was in the cabin."

Pauline nodded. "I agree. They quarreled, she likely hit him with something, he was dead, she dragged him to the rail and bundled him over it."

"How did she manage his dead weight? How do we prove any of that?" Nona asked.

"We'll ask to observe that balcony and question the people in the room next door. Somebody surely would have seen or heard something. The man was killed during daylight hours."

"Should we involve that security officer? Rita?" Nona asked. "She may already have the proof we're looking for."

"I didn't like the way she brushed us off."

"You should be used to that by now. Everyone always thinks

we're just two old busybodies who'll get in the way," Nona said. "It's not personal."

"You're probably right," Pauline agreed. "And yes, I think we should tell her."

Madelyn returned from the washroom, looking green. "I'm going to go to my cabin and lie down."

"One of us should come with you," Nona said, rising to her feet. "We don't want any further accidents."

Madelyn didn't object.

"Order me the chicken parm sandwich, I'll be right back," Nona said to Pauline, and followed Madelyn.

MADELYN'S ROOM was a mess when Nona entered—clothes and towels strewn everywhere. Madelyn stumbled to the bedside, and Nona asked, "You don't need my help to get under the covers, do you?"

Madelyn shook her head.

Studying the room, Nona asked, "I hope you don't mind if I look over the balcony while I'm here?"

While Madelyn flopped face down on the unmade bed, Nona darted to the balcony. Two loungers were placed on either side of a small table, which left little room for manhandling bodies. There's a possibility they'd been rearranged after the body was bundled over. But the positioning did not give evidence to such. There was no sign of movement on the balcony floor, nor was there anything stuck to the rail to suggest anyone had been pushed over.

Nona clutched the railing and peered over. It was a straight drop to the deck where the victim had landed. This was where the victim had fallen from. "Madelyn wasn't drinking to drown her sorrow," Nona whispered. She crept into the bedroom, where Madelyn was asleep and snoring like a freight train.

Nona scrutinized the floor tiles and carpeting of the whole suite swiftly. There were no bloodstains or signs of a struggle. The room was untidy but in a casual, lazy way, not a *fight to the death* kind of way. Letting herself out of the suite, she hurried back to Pauline, who was waiting in the restaurant.

The meal arrived just as Nona took her seat.

"Well?" Pauline asked, dipping her bread into the au jus.

"It has to be her," Nona whispered as the waiter brought another basket of bread and oil. "There was no sign of anyone being in there but the husband and wife. It's definitely a straight drop from their balcony, too."

"Then we must visit the security woman."

"As soon as we finish our lunch," Nona replied.

"Madelyn is taking her husband's death very hard," Pauline mused, as they ate their food.

"She had to phone their kids and tell them their father was dead," Nona replied.

Pauline nodded. "If there's a good side to being single through life, it's not having to do things like that."

WHEN THEY'D HAD their fill of lunch, the two sleuths set off for the security office on the lower deck of the ship. Rita was in the office, but she was as unwelcoming of their new suggestion as she had been of their last theory.

"You didn't have any doubts about what happened?" Nona asked Rita.

"Madam," Rita said, "people come on cruises, and they overindulge. Ships have many decks, and other high places, for people to fall from. Thankfully this situation isn't common, but *accidents do happen*. I think you'll find this case is the same. Besides, we've never had a murder."

"You *will* do some investigating now we've raised the possibility?" Pauline stated. She found Rita's calm responses frustratingly unsatisfactory.

"As I told you, we have procedures we follow," Rita said. "There's nothing you need to do. Now, please, return to your vacation and enjoy the cruise as much as you can after this unfortunate accident."

As Nona and Pauline walked back to the shaded deck, Nona asked, "She really doesn't want to check this out, does she?"

Pauline agreed, adding, "I wonder where Madelyn was, if she wasn't in the cabin with her husband?"

"We can't question everyone on board about whether they witnessed her at the time the crime happened," Nona pointed out.

"No, but we can ask Madelyn when she sobers up. We can wait outside her cabin before the evening mealtime and catch her then."

THEIR VIGIL outside Madelyn's cabin was tedious, and there was nothing casual they could say to passersby as they skulked around in the corridor. Nona let out a huge sigh of relief when Madelyn finally emerged.

Pauline put a hand to her chest. "Madelyn, fancy seeing you again so soon! We were just heading to our cabins to freshen up. Are you feeling better?"

"A bit," Madelyn said. "I'm going to try to eat something light. Hoping to settle my stomach."

"Why don't we join you," Nona replied, linking arms with Madelyn, who tried to wiggle out of Nona's grasp.

"I'm going to the buffet," Madelyn said.

"The buffet sounds wonderful," Pauline agreed, smiling. "We were looking for something light too. We tend to eat and drink too much on these voyages."

The three women soon filled their trays with "light" items, and Pauline and Nona led the way to a quiet table with a view out to sea. Madelyn glanced among the chairs and sat with her back to the view of rolling waves. Pauline grinned.

After some small talk about the early days of the cruise, Nona asked, "You said you weren't with your husband when he fell. Where were you?"

Pauline was afraid Nona had been too blunt, but Madelyn didn't skip a beat. "I was at a lecture," she said, "learning about an island excursion."

"Your husband wasn't interested?"

"He's never interested in doing anything fun," Madelyn said. "He said he wanted to contact his office. He'd arranged some time on the ship's radio phone. I assumed he'd be in the communications room, not in the cabin."

"Did he say why he wanted to talk to his office?" Nona asked.

"No, it was always the same with Chuck. Wherever we went, he just worked. He had no interest in anything else, really."

"And what was his work?"

"Oh, his department handles drug smuggling and terrorism," Madelyn said. "That's why I'm certain someone on board killed him."

"Wow," Nona cried. "That's not your average job. I'm surprised you're sharing that with us."

Madelyn nodded. "It's not an average job, and it scared me, to be honest. It still does. I guess it doesn't matter if you know, now that he's—" She sniffled, but her eyes were dry.

"Do you think he saw someone?" Pauline asked. "Did he mention anyone specific?"

Madelyn shook her head. "He never tells me anything. He can't..." She paused, and added, "Well, couldn't, you understand. It was when he said he wanted to call back to the office that I figured he must have seen something."

"Had there been any incidents on the cruise targeted against your husband?" Nona asked. "He wasn't the guy who fell climbing for coconuts, was he?"

"Chuck wasn't the *action man* kind of agent. More the *man at the computer monitor* sort of agent. That's why I think he saw someone, or something."

"If he was caught witnessing *someone* or *something*, your deduction would be a good *motive*, if nothing else," Nona replied.

Madelyn nodded. "But the security people say he'd drank too much and fell. There's no evidence of anyone else being involved."

"Was that like your husband?" Pauline asked. "To drink too much, I mean?"

Madelyn nodded. "He used to joke that we both liked to party, just in our own way. Me with other people, him alone. Chuck was afraid he'd blurt something out in conversation if he drank in public."

After escorting Madelyn back to her room, Nona and Pauline returned to their own cabin in silence.

"I believed her," Pauline said at last. "Did you?"

Nona nodded. "Which means we were wrong, again, and we've set that security woman on her needlessly."

"Rita won't do anything anyhow," Pauline said. "She must already have been aware of Madelyn's location at the time he fell, yet she didn't mention it when we told her to investigate."

"It's as you said," Nona replied. "She doesn't want us taking an interest and brushes us off in whatever way she thinks will get rid of us quickest."

"He wouldn't have let a person he'd spotted into his cabin," Pauline mused.

"The victim wouldn't have, you mean? He might, if he thought he could manage the situation."

"The wife said he wasn't a man of action, so that can only mean one thing—a woman?" Pauline replied.

"Exactly. If the person at the door was a woman, he might have had a false sense of security."

"Only if he could see she wasn't armed," Pauline said, frowning.

"Maybe the person he recognized had an accomplice, or multiple accomplices," Nona said. "The crew, for example. Chuck may have been getting set up to talk to his office back home when a cabin steward came in with fresh towels or whatever. He wouldn't have suspected anything odd about that, would he?"

"Maybe," Pauline replied. "Should we tell Rita we no longer suspect Madelyn?"

Nona nodded. "She'll say *I told you so.* I hate it when people do that." She plonked down on her bed and tossed her sun hat onto the pillows.

"She'll do it politely, so it won't feel so bad," Pauline said. "I'll do it, if it makes you feel better. It was mainly my fault we went off down that rabbit hole." Pauline placed her sun hat on the small side table and unbuckled her sandals.

"I think a quick nap might do me some good, clear my mind," Nona murmured, rolling over, not even taking the time to pop off her tennis shoes.

"I'll go find Rita, then," Pauline replied as Nona snored softly.

PAULINE TRACKED Rita down and told her of their change of mind about the case. Rita smiled in a way that set Pauline's teeth on edge. Though, as Pauline had predicted, Rita was gracious in her triumph.

"An accident, Miss Riddell, as I said."

"But wasn't he killed by a blow to the head before he fell?" Pauline asked.

"Who told you that?"

"Everyone was talking about it," Pauline replied airily.

"There is a contusion that may have happened before the fall," Rita said cautiously, "but he likely just stumbled and hit his head. Then, not realizing how serious the injury was, he went out on the balcony for air, became dizzy and fell over."

"There will be an autopsy when we return to port, won't there?" Pauline asked.

"Of course. As I keep telling you, we have procedures and we're following them. Now please forget all this and enjoy the rest of the cruise."

Pauline kept a watchful eye as she walked back to their cabin, pondering if any of the staff she passed could be the accomplice. Nona was showering when Pauline unceremoniously dropped onto her own bed and waited until the shower stopped. She began filling Nona in on what she'd learned from Rita.

Nona left the air vent on when she stepped out of the bathroom. "It's possible," she said, but her tone was unconvincing.

"Of course it's possible," Pauline agreed. "She'll say anything plausible to get rid of us. An autopsy will confirm the timeline of Chuck's injuries. Unfortunately, that won't happen till we're back in Miami."

"If it happens at all. I've had an idea," Nona said, slipping into her flip-flops. "We need to make a call ashore too." Nona winked, and Pauline groaned.

"Nona, we've been wrong on this twice now. We shouldn't involve others in our floundering."

"But I'm not wrong this time," Nona said, and she explained her plan to Pauline before they headed off to the communications room.

As the *Adonia* entered the port of Miami, police boats accompanied the pilot boat, and a small group of armed officers clambered aboard.

"It's as well for us the captain wasn't in on it too," Nona said, as the police swung from their boats into the open door in the ship's side and out of their sight.

"And it's as well for us their staff photos were good enough to find a match on the police databases," Pauline said.

"Face-matching technology is really getting good now," Nona said. "You'd need serious plastic surgery to outwit computers in this new twenty-first century."

"Chuck didn't need facial-recognition technology, just hours of watching videos of suspects," Pauline said. "He knew the woman right away."

"Do you think she killed him?" Nona asked. "I do."

Pauline shook her head. "I'm sure Rita was the one he recognized, so he'd never have let her into the suite. I think one of those two stretcher-bearers who carried his body away is most likely the murderer. In fact, I suspected at the time—their expressions were wrong, triumphant rather than somber."

"Maybe you're wrong and it was one of the men Chuck recognized," Nona replied. "We'll never really know for sure."

"You're right. We should be making our way back to the cabin to finish our packing," Pauline said.

Before they could leave the railing, however, an officer approached. "With the captain's compliments, ladies, he'd like you to join him in his suite."

The captain was waiting, with a police officer in full SWAT team gear as they were shown into the room.

"Our two super-sleuths," the captain said, introducing them to the police officer. They shook hands and accepted his thanks.

"How did you spot the killers?" he asked.

"We only suspected one—Rita," Nona said. "And that was because we made a mistake in identifying the victim. A mistake she seemed to agree with us and she shouldn't have."

The captain and police officer were taken aback at this frank admission of dubious detecting.

Pauline said, "We initially concluded the victim was the man who'd fallen from a tree on the beach during an excursion; we said so to the security woman"—she couldn't bring herself to use the woman's name now—"and she replied, 'accidents happen to men like him.'"

"When we said that, she just nodded, and we took that to mean she'd heard about the fall. Later, I remembered her expression looked odd to me. It was as if she didn't know what we were talking about and she was calculating what her response should be. I realized she'd only agreed with us so we'd accept the *accident* suggestion."

"Then," Nona interjected, "we were told by his wife the dead man had requested to use the ship's communication system to call his office and he was a government agent looking into drugs and terrorism. It was quite some coincidence he was killed before he could make that call. And who best to know who he was, and about his call back to his office, and stop him before he could raise suspicions, but the security officer?"

"Which is why you asked me personally for the use of the radio to contact the police in Miami," the captain said, "and asked me not to tell the security staff."

"Exactly," Pauline said. "And when we contacted our old police friends in Florida, they were able to get the right people involved, and here we are, and here you are." She indicated the police officer.

"They had a nice racket going here," the officer said. "The three principal officers in charge of security for the ship, passengers, and crew." He shook his head in disbelief. "There will be questions about how that happened on a ship that regularly sails in and out of the States, to and from dozens of countries where drugs are made."

"The cruise line has promised a substantial reward, ladies," the captain said. "I'm sure that will include a free cruise."

"Or two," Nona said, and winked at the captain.

He smiled. "I hope that means I'll have the pleasure of your company again?"

Her cheeks flushed. "I'm sure we'll cross paths in the future, Captain. Pauline and I live to travel now."

"And to investigate," Pauline added.

8

WAYLAID IN WISCONSIN

Ticket

THE MUSIC OF YESTERDAY

PRESENTING
THE
MAGNIFICENT
MACHINES
OF A
MAGNIFICENT ERA

P.C. JAMES
KATHRYN MYKEL

WAYLAID IN WISCONSIN

Mini Mystery #8

N ona shivered. "I can still feel the chill in my bones, Pauline. I thought Wisconsin had seasons, like New England. Why is it so darn cold?"

"It's September. What did you expect?" Pauline stood from the small breakfast table in the kitchenette of their luxurious hotel suite, and put the teakettle on the stove to boil. "We have time for tea before we head over to that monstrosity?"

"The *Cottage on the Cliff* and its collections of antiques is a *wonder*, not a monstrosity. Besides, it beats a football game. In an open-air stadium. In Wisconsin. In September!" Nona replied, her eyebrows raised and her eyes widening further after each statement.

"What are you going on about, *Gretta*? That was three days ago. Surely you must be warmed up by now." Pauline asked.

Sitting at the small round breakfast table in her bathrobe,

Nona shivered one more time and smiled. "*Miss Riddell,* we've been on a dozen vacations together, and you still insist on calling me by my given name!" Nona laughed. The two companions had a playful banter despite being polar opposites in every way.

"You must be all too familiar with open-air stadiums, being from Boston," Pauline commented.

"I'm from Salem," Nona corrected. "Yes, we have one too. I know you think the *Cottage* is a better idea than going to this circus." Nona tapped her perfectly manicured nail on the colorful flier she was holding.

The teakettle whistled, and Pauline placed two teacups on the table, with the tea bags already in the cups.

"Yes, I do, I don't care for the circus. Clowns are creepy. By the way, what exactly is a clown *vase* anyhow?" Pauline asked, having looked briefly at the flier earlier. She poured the steaming water into the two cups. "Is that an American thing? I was under the impression clowns piled out of *cars*, not vases?"

Nona smiled appreciatively as she wrapped her hands around her cup, careful not to touch it directly, but close enough to soak up the warmth radiating from the mug.

"I have no idea. I've never heard of such a thing. Normally they all climb out of one of those little buggies."

Pauline placed the kettle onto a cold burner atop the stove.

"I think I might like to see this 'ICP,'" Nona said, reading more of the flier and sipping the warm tea.

"What is 'ICP?'" Pauline asked, taking the seat across from Nona.

"Says here it stands for 'Insane Clown Pack.'"

"Then I know you're right. *Cottage on the Cliff* it is. I'd much rather have a nice, quiet day at a cottage than juggle a pack of insane clowns at the zoo." Pauline bristled, and sipped her own tea, her pinky finger poised upward.

Nona laughed and corrected her Canadian friend. "It's the circus, Pauline. Not a zoo."

They sat in silence for a few minutes, enjoying their tea. Nona donned her usual mischievous grin. "You should be happy to get out of this room, Pauline."

"Yes, I am, though I am still a little ambivalent about what we shall find at this next *tourist trap* of yours." Pauline looked past Nona, across the room. Her expression was one of dismayed amusement.

Knowing exactly what Pauline was looking at behind her, Nona said, "Hey, don't mock. My son will get a kick out of that cheese hat."

WHEN THEY ARRIVED at the *Cottage on the Cliff* property an hour later, their chauffeur parked the black town car and opened the door for the two women to scoot out. A whoosh of cold, crisp air hit Nona, followed by a deep woodsy scent. She breathed it in, and then coughed.

"Oh good, a view," Pauline commented, looking out over the thick wooded landscape. A puzzled look crossed her face, and she added, "This looks significantly bigger than a cottage on a cliff."

Laughing at her friend's cynicism, Nona said, "There have been multiple warehouse-size additions over the years. It's not called Cottage on the Cliff for nothing. In regards to the view, I mean."

Noticing there were no other cars in the small gravel parking area, Nona cheered, "Looks like we have the whole place to ourselves."

"Well, that's what we get with a paid guided tour, I guess.

That means we will be free to enjoy our trip, without a murder to solve!" Pauline said, with hope in her voice.

"You do realize that every time one of us says that, we end up finding a body!" Nona replied, then dropped her head at the inevitability that her friend had just jinxed them.

Pauline sighed and shrugged. "Maybe just this once, we won't!"

They both looked up as a short balding man approached. "Good day, ladies. My name is Claude, and we are thrilled to have you here at the Cottage on the Cliff." Dressed in bizarre finery that didn't quite fit his physique, he bowed to the women.

"Thank you. My name is Nona Galia." Nona held out her hand to shake, but the man took her outstretched hand and turned it. Bringing the back of her hand to his mouth, he planted a kiss on her long, slender fingers. Her eyes widened, and she turned to Pauline for backup.

Pauline stepped forward with her own hand extended and greeted the man. "I'm Miss Pauline Riddell." She didn't like the look of the man—or his attire, which wasn't befitting of a tour guide for an architectural site.

Instead of shaking or kissing *her* hand, he simply nodded at Pauline.

In the meantime, Nona had pulled out a tissue to wipe a smudge off her hand, but before she could finish, the man wrapped his arm through hers.

As Claude whisked her to the entrance of the cottage, Nona glanced back and gave Pauline a "help me" look.

Pauline shrugged and returned an "I tried" grin at Nona and followed them in.

"The cottage was designed by the famous architect, Alan Gordan." Claude began his spiel and swept one short arm towards the building. "As you can see, it is so much more than a humble cottage hanging off the side of a cliff."

Inside the entrance to the house, light filtered in through dark blue panels of the slanted glass windows that covered the room from floor to ceiling. The blue hue gave Nona the impression of an evening atmosphere, in stark contrast to the bright, sun-filled day they'd just left. The front door closed behind them with a thud.

Still clutching Nona's arm, Claude steered her through the first room of the house—a living room with display cases filled with ancient shoes and vintage toys. Peculiar items, like period hats, covered the nineteenth century couches. The room was chock full of *stuff.* Claude waved his left hand, signaling the continuation of their tour.

"I will be your . . ." He stopped short in front of a table display. "This can't be!" he exclaimed.

"What is it?" Pauline asked from behind them.

Nona turned her head to Pauline, giving her an "I told you so" look.

"I was just here in this room when you arrived..," Claude started with a look of horror on his face.

"And?" Nona asked, wiggling and finally breaking free of his grip.

"The Confetti Mica Marble is missing!"

"The what marble?" Pauline asked.

"A priceless game-playing marble. It's not your kids' schoolyard glass marble," Claude cried. "It's a real-deal marble."

"Maybe it rolled onto the floor?" Nona stated, scanning the tiled flooring. She then eyed Pauline and shrugged.

"Pff. Madam, you don't understand. I was doing inventory on the marble collection and we *three* are the only ones in here." He pointed between them and then stared back at Pauline.

"Well, don't look at me," Pauline exclaimed. "I have no use for a silly toy marble."

"Silly toy! You mock me, madam? This toy, as you describe it, is the rarest marble in the world. Its value is priceless."

Nona cleared her throat to get Claude's attention. "Well, not quite priceless, Claude. According to this plaque," she tapped on a wooden sign near the oval marble display case, "it's worth approximately twelve thousand dollars."

"Twelve thousand dollars, for a child's marble?" Pauline exclaimed.

"And to your comment, Claude," Nona said, "I haven't taken it either, so if it's only we three here, that leaves you." She paused, and continued triumphantly, "And you're the only one of us who even knew of its existence . . . and its value. Mystery solved."

"Hey," Claude cried, "quit pointing fingers."

"You started it," Nona snapped.

Claude's face was thunderous, but his tone was conciliatory. "I didn't mean to point fingers. The realization came to me, and I said it. I wasn't suggesting any of us did it."

"We're pleased to hear that," Pauline said. "But if we didn't, then who did?"

"That was my point," Claude said. "No one else could have taken it."

"Someone did," Nona said. "The question is who and how?"

"The exhibits aren't locked up or chained down," Claude replied.

"Maybe they should be, or at least in a case or under a cover," Pauline said. "If they really are that valuable."

"Is there a house cat or dog?" Nona asked. "Is the marble small enough that an animal could have mistaken it for food and swallowed it?"

"There's a cat," Claude answered.

"Well, where's this cat?" Pauline asked. "We should question it."

"Question the cat?" Claude asked.

After a brief search of the room, Claude led them out into a corridor that ran along the side of the house.

"Whoa, wait," Nona said. "Shouldn't you lock the entry door behind us? We don't need any more thefts while we're away."

Flustered, Claude turned back and did as Nona had suggested. They continued quickly along the corridor into a staff area hidden behind an inconspicuous door. A uniformed man, holding a pack of greasy playing cards, was seated at a small round lunch table, with a coffee cup and half-eaten sandwich next to him and a game of solitaire in progress. A startled look crossed his face, and he jumped from his seat when the group burst in.

"Where's the cat?" Claude asked.

"It's over there," the man said, pointing to a tawny cat lapping milk from an ornate porcelain water bowl. As he pointed, Pauline noticed on the arm of his uniform what appeared to be a security guard patch.

Claude lunged for the cat. The cat fled across the floor and under a chair. The cat's tail—sticking out—darted back and forth as if to taunt Claude. The feline let out a long caterwaul in response to Claude's second advance.

The security guard asked, "What are you doing?"

"We think the cat may have eaten the Confetti Mica Marble," Claude replied, desperately reaching under the chair as the cat escaped again and, with one leap, landed halfway up a curtain that hung from the ceiling.

Claude reached for the cloth but snatched his hand back.

"What's wrong now?" Pauline asked.

"It's a curtain from the dining room," Claude said. "A very valuable curtain, made of *silk,* from the *eighteenth century*."

"Well, that proves the cat has no respect for valuable items," Pauline said. "But does it prove the cat ate the marble?"

"This is no time for levity, madam," Claude replied. The cat was now perched on the rod that held the curtain up, hissing at Claude.

Nona chimed in, "It also proves the cat could easily have leapt onto the table where the marble was kept. Its first jump here was twice that height."

"We must get that cat x-rayed," Claude said. "We can't wait for nature to take its course. If it wasn't the cat, we need to know now, before the trail goes cold."

The security guard eyed Claude suspiciously. "Are you sure that's a good idea?"

"Where will we find x-ray equipment near enough and available enough to get a quick answer?" Pauline asked.

"Why, here, of course," Claude replied, his voice as shrill as the cat's caterwauling. "We use it for our preservation work on some of the rarer exhibits."

With the cat now entangled in the curtain, the guard said, "Then back off."

Claude backed up, and Nona and Pauline awkwardly shuffled closer to the door, avoiding Claude. When they had all backed up, the guard held up his open hand towards the cat. His long, thin fingers presented a small piece of meat.

The cat's desire for the treat finally overcame his natural tendency to flee, and the feline slowly, suspiciously clawed his way back down the curtain far enough to be gathered up in the guard's arms. A look of utter horror showed on Claude's face the entire time.

While the cat gingerly ate its reward, it began to purr, and the group proceeded to another room—laboratory-like and filled with curious objects, artifacts and strange equipment.

TEN MINUTES LATER, after more of the guard's sandwich and a whole lot of cajoling, they had their answer. The cat—whose name, they learned from his tag, was Chuckles—didn't contain the marble.

"Thanks, friend," Claude said, nodding to the wiry man who'd tamed the cat, as they returned to the staff room and replaced the cat in front of its milk bowl.

The man smirked, shaking his head, and sat in front of the card game.

Claude, Pauline, and Nona returned to the exhibit room to take a closer look at the scene of the crime.

"Well, we're back at square one." Pauline shrugged. She pursed her lips and narrowed her eyes as she looked around the room at the vignettes and tchotchke items. "There is so much"—she paused—"stuff."

Claude began to pace the narrow path from one end of the room to the other. The space looked like it had been taken over by a hoarder with very expensive taste.

"I think you are all missing the key clue here," Nona said with a clever grin.

Claude stopped pacing, and he and Pauline looked at Nona expectantly.

"Well, Claude, you said we *three* are the only ones here. So who was that man?"

A look of uncertainty crossed his face. "He's security, obviously. And I assure you he isn't our thief."

"And why not?" Pauline asked in a clipped tone.

Nona added, laughing at Claude's naïveté. "Have you never seen a heist movie? There is always an inside man, and often he, or she," she said, tilting her head condescendingly towards Claude, "is one of the *security* personnel."

"I can't fathom how you could dismiss him so easily," Pauline scoffed.

"Was he in this area during the time frame the marble vanished?" Nona asked.

"Madam, you make it sound like a magic trick. I assure you . . ."

Nona interrupted him. "Well, it could be sleight of hand, but that wasn't what I was getting at, per se."

"Well, spill already, Nona, so we can find the marble and get on with this tour," Pauline chided, reaching up to touch the curvature of a six-foot-tall blue porcelain vase.

"Do not touch. Please, ma'am," Claude said, pointing to a plastic sign that said exactly that.

Pauline's hovering hand snapped back to her side. "My apologies. I am simply mesmerized by the size of it. It's like the one on the circus flier."

"Earth to Pauline," Nona said, waving her hand. "We have a case to solve." Nona waited for Pauline to turn and show her attention and then repeated her question to Claude. "Was he in this area?"

"Well, yes, of course. He patrols the building."

"Were you in here when he last came through?" Nona asked.

Claude scratched his head. "No. I would be outside with you ladies."

Nona rolled her eyes. "I still don't understand why you said there was no one else here, Claude."

"I told you, he's security. I didn't think . . ."

"Tell us more about the security guy," Pauline demanded. She stepped closer to Claude. She eyed him, as if to take his measure, and asked, "How long has he been working here? Has anything else of value gone missing lately?"

"I assure you he's honorable, a friend even," Claude replied, and huffed before adding, "in good standing," as he backed away from Pauline.

"Well, what's the problem, then, Claude?" Nona replied,

stepping closer to him also. The two women flanked him; they had him caught in their trap.

He waved his hands furiously around. "Honestly, ladies, what are you getting at?" His eyes darted between the two women.

"What I'm deducing here, Claude, is it must have been you!" Nona smirked.

Pauline held up her index finger and waved her hand around in a circle. "I'm *circling* you as well. You lied about who was in the *ring*, you cleverly found the marble had been *hit*. You were the last one to account for it, *and* you say the other employee is upstanding. I'm *knuckling down* on *you* as the thief!" Pauline said with a triumphant smile on her face. "I *played* marbles as a child, you see."

Claude stood staring at Pauline, his eyebrows knitted, the expression of a shocked animal on his face.

"Good game, Pauline! Way to *shoot* the *lingo*. Who knew?" Nona marveled at her friend, who had just used nearly every marble game term in the book in one fell swoop.

"I may not know how much rare marbles *cost*, but I do know how to play the game." She nodded.

"Well, Claude?" Nona taunted. "What do you have to say for yourself?"

Claude's expression changed from dumbfounded to horrified. "You're madwomen," he replied. "Why would I even mention the marble was missing if I'd taken it?"

"To throw the blame on us," Nona snapped back, stepping even closer to him.

"Well, then, why would I have the cat x-rayed so quickly, knowing it would show the feline to be innocent?"

"For the same reason," Pauline replied.

The alarm on Claude's face was growing with each rebuttal. "And why would I say the guard was an honest man? All these things I've done, to try and *recover* the marble, point to my innocence, surely?"

Nona frowned. "My name is Nona, don't call me Shirley."

It certainly was strange behavior if he was guilty. He should have been creating suspicion everywhere, *if* he *was* the thief.

"Well," Nona said slowly, "they are points in your favor. But Pauline and I know it wasn't us, and you say it wasn't the guard, and we've eliminated the innocent cat, so who does that leave—but you?"

"I don't know," Claude said. "That's what we have to find out."

AFTER A CURSORY SEARCH of the room, Pauline and Nona regrouped.

"The difficulty is," Pauline said, looking around, "there's so much clutter in here that anyone could have hidden the marble. Or hidden themselves, even. They could still be here, lying in wait for us all to leave so they can make their exit with the marble."

"It's not clutter," Claude shrieked.

"Artifacts, then," Pauline amended. "You sure are an eccentric man, Claude."

"Pauline just means there are so many artifacts, anyone could be hiding among them, like in the huge vase, for example," Nona said quickly. His face was flushed, and beads of sweat were forming on his forehead.

"I assure you, no one is hiding in any vase."

"But maybe we should examine the guard," Nona said. "Just to be sure."

"You want to examine, as in x-ray, the guard?" Claude asked.

"Well, I, ah . . . I didn't necessarily mean 'x-ray' him. Maybe check his belongings," Nona suggested.

"Then let's call him here and hear what he has to say for himself," Pauline urged.

"What about skylights or windows?" Nona asked, peering around, as Claude hurried off. "We speculated about the cat, but what about a raccoon? Curious beasts. One could have climbed in from outside?"

"A raccoon wouldn't take just one item and leave everything neat and tidy and untouched, though," Pauline replied.

"It might, if something about the item caught its attention," Nona said, walking the length of the room, scanning the ceiling. She stopped at the vase and tapped lightly. A hollow "ting" echoed in the air. "Worth a shot," she murmured. "I suppose it could be an animal, but I think it would have knocked some of this stuff over in the process." She glanced around, dismayed.

"Maybe a crow? A crow would extract just one shiny item." Pauline waved at a display of old spectacles and monocles. "They do like shiny things. A marble qualifies as a shiny thing." Pauline's lips pursed, and her brow wrinkled. "What about the open-window theory? Maybe a child could climb in. A child would spy the marble as desirable for its own sake, not for the value of it."

"There are no windows that would open," Nona replied. "And never mind how—you'd have to be an aerial acrobat to get down to it. But *why* would a child be out here alone on the cliff?"

"Okay, not a child." Pauline stopped pacing. "A small person, like a circus character? After all, the circus is in town so why not?"

Nona laughed. "I think you mean circus *performer*. You know, this reminds me of our California Adventure." Nona surveyed the small room. "If we could just get to the walls, maybe we could tap on them to check for a secret passage or trapdoor?"

"There's too much stuff. It's everywhere." Pauline pointed to a large display of vintage women's hats on the wall beside her. Under the display of hats, a bench ran the length of the room. "We can't even sit down on anything." She picked up a vintage throw pillow, and dust filled the air, causing them both to cough and sneeze. "My money is still on Claude or the guard," Pauline noted, "but we can try and..."

Before she began searching, Nona looked up to check on Pauline's unfinished sentence. Claude had returned with backup, the guard, and was now covering Pauline's mouth as she struggled against the hold on her arm.

"Unhand her, you, you, you scoundrel," Nona cried, lapsing into theatrical language that suited all that was happening.

"You're coming with us, ladies," the guard said as he advanced on Nona, grabbed her by the arm and got her purse in one swift move.

"I knew it was *you*! Unhand us," Nona yelled at the two men, failing to break free of the guard's grip.

They marched Pauline and Nona down the long corridor and sat them on cold metal chairs. Not in the break room they'd visited previously. This new room was darkened with blacked-out windows, and the air was musty.

"Hand over the marble, and we'll let you go," Claude demanded. A look of insincerity crossed his face before he fixed his eyes on Nona.

"As if," Nona scoffed.

After tossing their purses onto a table in the corner of the room, Claude struggled with the tiny zipper on Nona's purse, his clumsy fingers eventually moving the delicate closure.

"Hey! Get your grubby mitts off my purse," Nona yelled. "How long are you going to keep up this charade?" She tried to stand. A strong, beefy hand on her shoulder stopped her from rising. She looked up at the offender and snarled, "We know it was you two buffoons who stole the marble. There's no way you're pinning it on us."

Nona continued to struggle under the pressure of the guard's grip.

Pauline spoke calmly. "Let's be logical here, Claude. You think we're the thieves, but it most certainly was not us. We think you're the culprit, and you claim that to be a false conclusion. So, I propose we work together to find the true crook."

Claude stopped rifling through the women's purses, and Nona added. "We can't search the whole place unless you plan on calling in the authorities. So *we* need to search that room again."

Claude's expression changed to one of contemplation, and he put his hands on the edge of the table. Leaning against it, he stared straight at Pauline. "Fine. But first, we must check your purses *and* your pockets, just to be sure."

"You will not put your hands on us or our belongings again, or we'll be calling the authorities immediately," Pauline said fiercely, and nodded to Nona.

"Fine, then empty your pockets and bags, and once we're satisfied, we'll search," Claude replied.

Pauline dug in her pockets and patted her slacks flat. "See? Nothing."

Nona pulled out a small package of tissues and her cell phone from her left pocket and shrugged.

"Now the other pocket, lady," Claude demanded.

She reached into her pocket and pulled the lining out with her fingertips to show there was nothing in it.

"Now your bags," Claude demanded.

They did as he asked and proved there was nothing that shouldn't be there.

"All right, now we'll all go and search the room. Together,"

Claude agreed, and motioned for the women to stand up. "You two first, where I can see you."

Pauline gave Nona a pointed look and high-tailed it out of the dark room. Nona was allowed to follow Pauline down the corridor until it led back to the living room where the case of the missing marble had begun.

There was hardly enough room for the four searchers to pass around one another as they searched the room. Nona cornered Pauline near the entrance and whispered, "I have the marble."

"Whaaat?" Pauline cried out, too loudly, and they both looked up. Neither man was paying attention, their backs to the two women.

"Shh," Nona whispered.

"Is this some spy activity that I wasn't aware of?" Pauline whispered.

Nona blinked. "I have no idea what you are talking about."

"Well then what do you mean, *you* have the marble? *You* stole it?" Pauline asked.

"No. Of course not," Nona retorted, shaking her head. "One of them must've slipped it into my pocket back there."

They both looked across the room. Claude was gone.

"Hey, where's Claude?" Nona shrieked.

"You must find him," Pauline yelled at the guard still standing there. "Claude's the thief!"

After he rushed off, Nona replaced the marble in its holder. "I had a hunch this whole *missing marble caper* was nothing but a ruse."

"Why? How? How did you know it was a trick?" Pauline questioned.

"I didn't *really* know. I just had a hunch, I guess." She shrugged. "Look, Claude and the guard are gone, and the marble is back. Let's get out of here before things go bad." Nona grabbed Pauline's arm.

"We have to tell someone, Nona," Pauline said. "We can't just leave."

"Do you want to be forcefully detained again when the guard realizes the marble is back and I was the one who had it? He's not going to believe my word that it was his friend Claude."

"We'll contact a manager or the owner," Pauline said, leading the way back to the entrance.

"Or the authorities?" Nona added.

"We will have *our* story told first."

At the front entrance, they were not surprised to find the ticket office unlocked and they let themselves in. Rummaging around, they found a phone and a list of employee numbers. When they'd finally managed to contact someone in charge of the property, it took some convincing.

"We don't have a guide called Claude," the man said.

"You must, the security guard knew him," Nona exclaimed.

He said, "I'll be there in twenty minutes." An obnoxious dial tone rang in Nona's ear.

"I hate when people hang up on me." Nona turned to Pauline. "He's on his way. I'm miffed we spent so much time caught up in this caper as the patsies," Nona added.

Pauline opened the front door. "Let's wait outside, it's too stuffy in this place."

The two duped sleuths stepped out into the sun; a car, too far off to read its license plate, was racing down the road. A cloud of dust hung in the air behind it.

"Claude, you think?" Nona asked.

"Probably," Pauline replied. "We can describe the car to the manager when he gets here. If anything valuable has gone missing, they might be able to catch him."

"We were supposed to be the scapegoats."

Pauline nodded. "Claude steals something more valuable but fits us up with the marble. The police waste their time trying to make us crack, and he gets far away with whatever it is he really stole."

AN OLDER GENTLEMAN ARRIVED, not at all what Nona had been expecting, from the curious look on her face when he walked up and greeted them. "Ladies," he said, and nodded for them to follow. "We'll find the guard and get to the bottom of this."

He led them through the main entrance and in a different direction than they'd gone at the start of the tour, causing Pauline to ask, "Is this the way to the security guard's office?"

"It sure is, why?"

"Because it isn't where we were taken previously," Nona replied.

After a long walk down an endless hallway, they arrived at a door marked "Security," and the manager knocked and entered without waiting for a response. He stopped halfway into the empty room. "Must be on his rounds," he muttered as Nona halted, just short of knocking into the man.

Nona gave Pauline an innocent look. "Oops."

"Nona," she grumbled, and hustled to catch up to the departing manager.

"Do you know where he'll be?" Pauline asked, struggling to keep up with his pace.

"I know his route. We'll meet him on his way back."

They continued for a few moments along a corridor in a silence broken only by the clip-clop of their own shoes on the floor and then a faint shuffling.

"Did you hear that?" Nona asked.

"Hear what?"

They listened for a moment, and a curious thumping came

from behind them. "That doesn't sound like the usual house noises of machinery or musical instruments that reverberate through the building," the manager said.

"So what is it?" Nona asked, and turned an ear towards an unmarked door.

They pushed the door open, only to find the security guard neatly trussed and gagged in a small closet of cleaning paraphernalia.

"What happened to you, George?"

The manager bent and ripped the duct tape from the guard's mouth, who screamed, "Two men jumped me!"

"Must've been Claude and the imposter security guard. The same two who came up with the stolen marble scheme," Nona replied.

"They stole the marble?" George asked as Pauline cut the binding around his hands with her pocketknife.

"No, they slipped it into my pocket before they escaped," Nona replied.

"Well, that's a curious move," George said, standing on shaky legs. The manager helped him out of the closet. "A ruse to steal something else? Or a double cross, you think, Silas?"

"I think we should check on that marble," the manager, Silas, replied.

All four made a beeline for the front room, wedging themselves across the width of the hallway before the manager squeezed ahead, leaving the two amateur sleuths to follow him and the real security guard.

Silas breathed a sigh of relief at the sight of the marble cradled in its holder. "I guess they decided with you two knowing what they'd done, they'd just put everything back and run."

"Not so fast," Nona chimed in. "I'm with George on the ruse to steal something else."

"I agree." Pauline added, "I think you should check all the small valuable objects in the collections."

"Who are you two, anyway?" the manager asked suspiciously.

"We're renowned sleuths, but that doesn't matter right now," Nona replied. "Let's discover if anything more valuable is missing."

"This place is huge, and there are a lot of valuable items in the house. But not many anyone could walk out with," the manager said, as they made their way to the next room.

"Well, the marble was left out where someone could steal it."

"An oversight for sure," Silas responded, his tone firm until he cried out, "Oh no!"

When they entered the next room, he was staring at the blank place in an open cabinet. "The Romanov Egg is gone."

Pauline inspected the lock on the curio. "It's been muscled open, that's for sure."

"Ladies, I appreciate your assistance, but I must contact the authorities now, and you must wait until they arrive."

The police interviewed each of them, remaining unimpressed by the sleuths' story and their suspicions concerning Claude and the guard.

BACK IN THE safety of their suite, Nona chattered with her mouth full of cheese curds. "Do you think they believed us at all?"

"I think they consider us suspects," Pauline replied, "even though we showed them that our clothes, bags and car were completely egg-free."

"I hope they catch that car," Nona murmured. "But we can't

just let this go. Claude is in the wind. I knew the whole marble thing was a smokescreen to steal something else."

"That Romanov Egg is extremely valuable, and not just for the gold and gems it's made of."

Reaching for a napkin to wipe her mouth, Nona spilled her apple juice. Pauline shoved the pile of napkins in her direction. Cleaning up the spilled juice, Nona spied the circus flier they'd been discussing previously.

With a twinkle in her eye, Nona opened her mouth, but Pauline shut her down. "Don't even say it, I know what you are thinking."

"Are you game for some kettle corn, elephant ears and cotton candy for dinner?" Nona grinned at Pauline.

"Yuck, that stuff will rot your gut. That's not a proper dinner for anyone. Besides, you're too old for cotton candy."

"Nonsense, I'm not too old for anything!"

Pauline grimaced. "Okay, but what will we find at the circus? At night? Besides that 'Insane Clown Pack?'"

Nona finished off the curds before gulping the last of her juice while Pauline sipped her tea.

Nona finally spoke, reading from the brochure. "Siamese twins, purloining aerialists, and Clive Stolethesho, the renowned ringmaster of Wisconsin's Chez Cirque du Fromage."

Pauline tilted her head at her friend with a confused look.

"Yeah, I can't believe I said that without laughing!" Nona replied.

"I don't even know what you just said. Translation?"

Nona tapped the flier. "What? I was just reading it from the flier."

"How does this fit in with the investigation?"

"'Claude the Clown' is how," Nona replied.

"We don't know that, though he looks a bit like one. I think *you're* acting like a clown. We should definitely leave this one up to the police."

"We say that every time, and we've never taken our own advice."

"They'll think we're mad for sure this time." Pauline scowled.

Nona shook her head. "No, they won't. Besides, it's the *circus*, it'll be fun."

"Fine, but those snacks you mentioned, if they're even edible, you're buying," Pauline replied. "And I might still require a proper dinner."

A SHORT TAXI RIDE LATER, the two women stepped out into a cacophony of sounds, sights and smells—sounds: bells, hawkers and roaring tigers; sights: flashing lights, cheese hats and men on stilts; smells: burnt sugar, animal manure and fried food.

A tall man on stilts crossed in front of the pair, nearly clipping Nona's arm as she pointed towards the ticket booth.

"Geez, watch where you're going, buster," Nona yelled, before pulling Pauline forward. "Did he look familiar?"

"No, and I don't see how he could've been someone we know," Pauline replied.

At the booth, Nona said, "Two tickets, please."

"That'll be thirty dollars," the young girl said, behind a popping bubble of gum.

Nona waited, staring at Pauline expectantly.

Pauline fished out her wallet. "Does that include a senior discount?"

She handed the money through the little slot in the ticket booth, and the girl said, "That'll be twenty-eight dollars, please."

Shuffling beside the booth, Nona questioned, "That's it, only two dollars?"

"Yes, ma'am."

Pauline scooped up the two-dollar bill and the tickets. Handing a ticket to Nona, she said, "For the scrapbook. Where do you want to start?"

Nona frowned, puzzled by Pauline's inane question.

"I know, food. But we're here on *your* hunch," Pauline quipped.

"Okay, let's review what we know."

"Not much. We've been involved in a charade to cover up the theft of a rare egg," Pauline replied.

"And there are at least two conspirators, both in the wind," Nona added.

"What made you think we would find answers here at the circus?"

"Claude was wearing a costume and makeup. I'm sure of it."

"I didn't notice any makeup." Pauline raised one eyebrow. "Only weird clothes."

"I think he was wearing lipstick? I wiped it off my hand when he—" The words *kissed my hand* went unsaid, but her scrunched up face communicated plenty. "How about we check out the clowns first? It might be quite entertaining to see how many they fit into that giant vase, like on the brochure."

Pauline grumbled, "If we must."

Walking into the big top area, Nona turned left and said, "I still can't believe they only gave us one dollar off for the senior discount. How does that help?" She spun around when Pauline didn't reply to her rant. To her surprise Pauline wasn't behind her.

"Where'd she go?"

Scanning the crowd, she found Pauline near the stage and

hustled to her side. Nona wiggled her eyebrows and pointed to a sign on the back of the tent. "I have an idea."

"That says, 'Clowns Only.' No way!" Pauline replied.

"What better way for us to find Claude than joining the circus?"

MINUTES LATER, after they'd donned big red noses and multicolored wigs, Nona was teetering trying to fit into one of the polka-dot clown suits.

"You look ridiculous, Pauline," Nona said.

A tall performer, resplendent in a glittering red jacket, walked in and exclaimed, "What do you two think you're doing?"

Pauline looked to Nona, who looked back at Pauline, her lips closed tight as a clam. Pauline replied with a straight face, "The agency sent us over."

"The show is starting in two minutes. Get your suits on, and let's go. You need to be in that vase before the bell rings." He pointed to a set of steps that led to the top of the vase before making his way out of the clown area. Out of sight, he shouted at another tardy performer.

"If it's starting soon, Claude needs to get off those stilts we saw him on and be the clown we suspect him to be," Nona said, as they climbed the steps.

"What do you mean?" Pauline asked as she wriggled into the vase.

"When we came in," Nona said, dropping down to Pauline's side. "Didn't you notice the man on stilts?"

"You think it was Claude?"

"I'm sure it was," Nona replied. "It's hard to tell under the greasepaint, nose and wig, but I'm sure it was him."

Pauline, still looking to escape, asked, "There are no steps *inside*. How do we get out?"

"There'll be a way," Nona said briskly. "We've all seen this trick. The vase will be wheeled out into the ring. The magician will place a cloth over the top of the vase, where his assistants— that's you and me—are hiding. Then, at the climax, and after a lot of magic words, he pulls away the cloth, and the assistants step out to great applause."

No sooner had Nona spoken than what looked like a cloth was draped over the neck of the vase. "It's starting," Nona said excitedly. "Soon, they'll roll us into the ring. You'll see."

"But we haven't been shown how to get out when he pulls away the cloth," Pauline objected.

"It will be so obvious, even untrained amateurs like us will see it, I'm sure."

Above their heads a solid lid landed with a thud, and the last vestiges of light were extinguished.

"I don't think that is part of a trick," Pauline said. "I suggest we call for help."

After a moment of shouting as hard and loud as they could, Nona said, "Listen how quiet it is when we stop yelling." Not a sound of the outside world penetrated the thick walls or cover of the vase.

"Make me a foothold, Pauline, with clasped hands. I'll reach up and push the lid off."

Pauline scoffed, "I really must be out of my mind." She clasped her hands and put them out. "How you conned me into this clown suit, never mind into this vase, I'll never know."

Nona felt around in the dark for Pauline's hands, then carefully placed her foot and pushed up.

The lid, however, didn't move even with her hardest pressing. Nona stepped down, falling against the wall of the vase. "Maybe you try, Pauline," Nona said, using the vase to secure her stance. "Here's my hands. Step up, bracing yourself against the side."

When Pauline couldn't move the lid either, she asked, "Do you think Claude means for us to die here?"

"I'm sure he just needs time to escape," Nona said, in what she hoped was an optimistic tone. "I guess he recognized us, but don't worry. He'll leave a message, and we'll be rescued. He won't want our deaths on his hands."

"This vase isn't very big. There can't be many hours of oxygen in it with us taking up so much space."

"We should sit and conserve, then," Nona said, "while we plan our escape."

They sat quietly in the dark for a few minutes, before Nona asked, "Do you have your sling bag under that clown suit? Maybe there's something we could use to bang on the walls with."

"I have your knitting needles," Pauline said. "I never thought I'd be glad to be carrying them around."

"Do you think these will make a louder sound than our hands and feet?" Nona asked.

"If we rat-a-tat Morse code, it might make a sharper, higher note than our feet and hands, and someone might recognize it isn't a natural sound and come looking."

Using the heads of the metal needles clasped in her hands, Pauline hammered on the wall as hard as she could. She tapped out an SOS message and waited silently.

Suddenly, the lid was lifted, and a flashlight shone in. "What are you two doing in there?" a man asked.

"We were told to get in there," Pauline said crossly, "and I suspect by friends of Claude."

He threw a rope ladder down, and the two sassy sleuths

climbed out. On the other side of the nearby tent wall, the circus was now in full swing.

"Well," the man demanded, when they were both once again on the solid earth, "who are you, and why were you in the magician's prop? We need to wheel it out into the ring, and you're holding up the show."

"We're sleuths on the trail of your clown," Nona said. "Where is he now?

"He's somewhere about," the man said. "He's on in fifteen minutes."

"Where would he wait?" Nona asked.

The man looked at her as if she were a madwoman. "How should I know?"

"You must know," Pauline said. "Even a circus must have a staging area for performers ready to go on stage."

Muttering under his breath, the man led them through the darkened area behind the entrance to the ring. Pauline had guessed correctly; clowns, a magician and his assistant, and various animals were preparing to burst into the ring. There was no sign of Claude, though.

"There he is," Nona cried, pointing outside through a gap in the tent wall to where a clown on stilts was hurrying away towards the fairground entrance.

They waddled off in pursuit, as fast as the ridiculous clown outfits would allow.

They'd barely left the tent when Pauline tripped and fell in a heap of fabric, losing a shoe. She tugged off the shoe from her other foot and clambered up onto her socked feet. Rushing to catch up with the man, Nona also tripped and sprawled out in front of the onrushing Pauline and Pauline toppled over Nona.

"Stop fooling around, Pauline," Nona urged. "Get after him."

Squeezing her arm, a man in cowboy clothes asked Pauline, "Are you okay, lady? You need a hand?"

"Of course I do," Pauline started, then eyed the rope looped over his shoulder. "Do you do lassoing?"

"Sure do, ma'am," he said. "I do everything there is to be done with ropes. Show me the beast, and I'll have it tied before you can say lickety-split."

"Then capture that clown," Pauline cried, pointing at Claude, who was getting away as fast as the stilts would let him.

"Or those stilts," Nona added.

"Sure thing," the cowboy said, and loped off in pursuit. Each holding their breath, the two sleuths watched as he began whirling weighted ropes above his head as he ran.

"A bolas," Pauline said, "just the thing."

The weighted, rope weapon whirled across the diminishing gap between the cowboy and Claude, before wrapping itself around the stilts. The stilts stopped, but Claude continued on, only now in an ungraceful arc, landing with a thumping face-plant on the grass next to the fun house. He scrambled out of his clown pants and was ready to run when a lasso looped over his head, and he was pinned in place. Pauline laughed at Claude, who was in a clown costume from waist to head, boxer shorts and socks from the waist down.

By the time Nona and Pauline caught up, Claude was neatly trussed and complaining adamantly about his treatment.

"Where's the egg?" Nona demanded.

"I don't know what you're talking about," Claude spluttered. "I'm a circus clown, what do I have to do with eggs?"

"You're not fooling anyone, buster," Nona said. "We were there. You tried to frame me with that marble so we'd take the blame when it was discovered that the Romanov Egg was stolen."

Claude stopped struggling, visibly deflated. "I don't have it," he said. "Gordo the sword swallower must have taken it."

By now there was a crowd gathered around the sleuths, the

cowboy and their captive. Nona shouted, "Someone call the police."

"Where might Gordo run to?" Pauline demanded, glaring at Claude.

"I can answer that," the cowboy said. "We shared a trailer at the last stop. He has family right here in town."

"He's probably been planning this for years, then," Nona said. "Waiting for the time to strike."

"Waiting for me to be his sucker," Claude griped. "He told me we were stealing the marble. I didn't know anything about the egg, believe me."

"Why should we?" Pauline asked.

"Because it's the truth," Claude said. "You telling me about the egg was the first I'd heard of it. I'd never have snitched on him otherwise."

FIFTEEN MINUTES LATER, the wailing siren of police cars grew louder until a car pulled up alongside the spectacle. An officer stepped out of the first car.

"Hey, cowboy," Nona shouted. "Tell the officer what he needs to know about Gordo the sword swallower."

Towing Claude behind him, the cowboy approached and explained to the officer who Gordo was and where he could be found.

The police officer eyed them all skeptically. Nona and Pauline explained quickly, too quickly, and had to repeat it a second time when the officer initially refused to believe them. Eventually, he radioed the description of Gordo's car.

He dropped the radio and asked, "And the man you're holding doesn't have this missing egg?"

"I haven't stolen anything, Officer," Claude cried. "I'm being held illegally by these people."

The officer shook his head. "Let him go," he said. "I'll take him in, and we'll do this properly."

"It's not in my possession," Claude shouted.

"And if that's true, you have nothing to worry about," the officer said, "though it sounds like you were complicit."

"I was used," Claude said. "I'm a victim. Not a villain."

The officer ushered him into the back of the police car and was about to slam the door shut when a call came through on the radio.

Pauline and Nona listened closely. ". . . the sword swallower was apprehended earlier. He had a box, but when opened, it was just metal junk. He claims to know nothing about any 'egg'. . ."

"Who else could it be?" the officer asked.

"The manager," Nona and Pauline said together. "You have to get over to the *Cottage on the Cliff* and stop him from escaping."

"Whoa, ladies," the officer said. "First you thought it was the clown, then the sword-swallower and now the manager. We can't just arrest people you think may have stolen things. There has to be a good reason before the police apprehend suspects."

"He must've set the two performers up, while he ran off with the egg."

"You'll have to explain better than this," the officer said. "I'll never persuade my boss to stop the manager of *Cottage on the Cliff* with what you've just said."

"We don't know all the details," Nona said. "But this is how we think it went. The manager probably knows this Gordo guy and they conspired to steal the Romanov Egg. Gordo knew Claude and paid him to show us around while the security guard was tied up."

"If they'd just taken the egg," Pauline interjected, "suspicion would have centered on the staff and especially the manager.

When we booked a guided tour, they had the perfect opportunity to steal the egg and make us the scapegoats."

"By planting the marble on us," Nona continued, when Pauline paused for breath. "The police would assume we'd stolen both and hidden the egg before we were caught."

"They expected we'd be frightened by what was happening and leave when they left us alone," Pauline said, recovering her breath and the initiative. "They didn't know we're sleuths, of course. We don't run away from strange cases. It's up to us to get to the truth."

"But why the manager?" the officer asked. "Why not just the two men you met?"

"Because they both claim not to have it," Nona said. "You've searched Gordo's car, and it wasn't there. Claude was genuinely shocked when he heard about the egg. I don't think he was truly in the gang—just the actor who played the guide."

"The manager and Gordo were the masterminds," Pauline said. "I'm guessing the manager seized the opportunity to point the finger at us, and when that didn't hold water, Claude would be the perfect patsy. And when *that* case collapsed, Gordo would hold the line, believing the manager was still going to split the proceeds with him."

The officer nodded. "Sounds like a stretch, but I'll call it in."

"The manager will be over the border in Canada by now," Pauline added gloomily. "He's had hours, if he fled right away."

"We can hold and search him at the border, if the powers-that-be think this hunch of yours has enough credibility. I'm not so sure they will," the officer said, before talking on the radio. His supposition was right. Headquarters did think this was an unlikely story.

"Look, this isn't a joke," Nona cried. "Tell them! Someone has that egg. We have one suspect here, you have Gordo, and there's a third, the manager, and he's out there somewhere."

THE NEXT DAY, Nona and Pauline visited the police station, demanding to know if the manager had been caught. "Well, ladies," the police officer said, "it seems your hunch was correct. Silas had the egg with him when we stopped him before the border."

"He knew Gordo and Claude, right?" Nona said.

"Went to school with Gordo—not his real name, by the way. Thick as thieves, they say. But contrary to popular belief," the officer said, "there's no honor among thieves."

"The egg is okay, is it?" Nona asked.

"It wouldn't have been worth so much if it had been damaged," the officer said. "He had a buyer lined up and everything."

"I guess that's why they had to distract us," Pauline said. "Our boasting about being sleuths had something to do with that. It was quick thinking on his part to see how he could use that to his advantage."

"And his next step was to use Gordo as a decoy," Nona said.

"You arrived at a bad moment for him," the officer agreed. "The plan was going nicely. The plan was to place the marble on you so when your tour was over and you were back in your hotel, the manager would find and untie the real guard, discover the missing marble and call the police. The police would find the marble and arrest you. When the manager would later discover the egg was also gone, you would be believed to have taken that also."

"But we wouldn't have the egg," Nona reminded him.

He nodded. "They thought we'd assume *you* hid it somewhere to keep it safe until the search died down. The marble is just petty theft, and you would claim you didn't know you had it.

You'd get away with it but muddy the waters so we couldn't see them through the murk."

"Meanwhile, his two accomplices would walk out with the egg and be well away before we all get caught up in this distraction around the marble," Pauline mused, before adding, "And it would be even longer before the egg was discovered missing. Maybe the next day, when the guard did his morning rounds. By then, the egg would be in the hands of an unscrupulous buyer."

Nona jumped in. "None of them would be suspected, our two circus artists would be in the afternoon performance, and the manager would be home having dinner with his family."

Pauline frowned. "Why wasn't he able to get away with the egg? He had lots of time."

"The officers who answered his call and interviewed you, kept him at the cottage too long," the officer said. "So you see, your involvement was instrumental everywhere. Thanks to your sharp eyes and wits, and your interest in seeing the mystery through, a valuable object remains on public display and not in some private collection. I'm sure the *Cottage on the Cliff* will want to thank you also."

"Well," Pauline said, as they left the station, "at least this time no one was murdered."

"It's not as exciting without a murder," Nona grumbled.

"I thought being suffocated in a vase was exciting enough, thank you. What can we do to take our minds off this? And don't say the circus," Pauline said, in a warning tone.

9

VACATED IN VANCOUVER

P.C. JAMES
KATHRYN MYKEL

VACATED IN VANCOUVER

Mini Mystery
#9

The marvelous photos they'd seen of Vancouver in full springtime bloom drew the traveling companions, Nona Galia and Pauline Riddell, to western Canada. They both had traveled west for this vacation—Nona from Boston, USA, and Miss Riddell from Toronto, Canada.

It was their first afternoon, and they weren't disappointed—the bright spring sunshine and Vancouver's flowers lifted their spirits after the long northern winters of their homes.

The glories of Mother Nature were short lived, though, as they woke the next day to a cold and misty, damp morning. Always in favor of making the best of their time together, the two friends crafted a plan to leave the knitting and quilting behind and bundle up for a walk. A ten-kilometer walk around Stanley Park, which they spied from their hotel window.

"How far is ten kilometers?" Nona asked, her voice filled with suspicion.

"About six miles," Pauline replied, in what she hoped was a cheery, encouraging tone. She really wanted to take a walk on this day that reminded her so much of her days at the seaside as a child.

"I'm not a great walker. I'm not sure how much longer these seventy-something-year-old bones are going to keep up with my twenty-five-year-old spirit," Nona grumbled, but her voice conveyed that she was up for the challenge.

"We'll make stops at the cafés and at the lookouts." The two sleuths headed out of the hotel and off to the narrow strip of land that connected Vancouver to Stanley Park.

"We must start with the totem poles," Pauline said. "I read about them in the guidebook."

"I think those things are creepy."

"They're harmless, Nona, you'll see." They continued in silence until they arrived at the grove where the totems stood in an arc, facing the visitors and the sea. Sea mist rolled in, obscuring their view of the city. Even the park's trees and bushes appeared and disappeared before them like phantoms.

"Is it safe to continue on?" Nona stood back.

"I'm confident the sun will soon burn it off."

"I thought they'd be bigger," Nona commented, at the totems.

A quiet peace surrounded the park, while the bustling city of Vancouver was far in the distance across the bay.

"They don't make trees the way they used to," Pauline quipped, smiling. "Why, when I was young, totem poles towered above me."

"They don't have totem poles in England, do they?" Nona asked, in her usual curious tone.

"Only fake ones and they're not made by any native

peoples of Britain," Pauline replied. "I was just saying, when we're young, things look bigger because we're so much smaller."

"Well, we *are* shrinking the older we get. I used to be five foot six. Now, I am lucky to reach the shelves at the market."

Pauline stood in awe of the totems, chuckling internally, while Nona contemplated her loss in stature.

"Are they like an ancient temple or just a tourist attraction?" Nona asked. "Stonehenge, that's what I'm thinking of. They remind me of Stonehenge."

"I expect they're exactly like that in real life, but this is just art displayed in the city park," Pauline said.

"So it's a tourist attraction," Nona mumbled as she stared. "If we touched them, would we go into a mysterious religious trance? Or become possessed? Like what happens in the movies?" Nona teased Pauline.

"Why don't you try, I suspect any power these totems possessed would be purely natural from the trees and the earth from which they sprang from, not supernatural."

They walked a few steps across the freshly cut grass until Nona was within touching distance of the tallest of the totem poles. She extended her hand towards the pole, then yanked it back. After a moment's hesitation, she reached out again. Her fingertips brushed the wood. Jerking her hand back, she cried out, her voice disappearing into the swirling sea mist.

"You're not fooling anyone, Nona," Pauline said, grinning. Nona was always up to shenanigans.

"You touch it," Nona said, taking a long, deep breath.

Pauline, shaking her head to show she didn't believe her friend's antics, reached out and grabbed the pole with both hands. Like everything else touched by Vancouver's wet climate, the totem was slick, damp and freezing cold. The grooves where the tools had worked the surface were smooth in contrast to the roughness under her palms, where nature had done its own work over the years.

"Well?" Nona asked.

"Well, what?"

"You didn't see anything?"

"No," Pauline said, her eyes widening with alarm. "What should I have *seen*?"

Nona touched the surface again and flinched, but this time her palm remained against the pole. "I saw a clandestine crime. A murder," she said in a slow, flat voice, her eyes focused somewhere far off.

Only a few passersby walked the main path near the service road.

"Where did you see the murder?" Pauline queried, still not sure if Nona was trying to pull one over on her.

"Here," Nona replied, her voice flat and emotionless. She stood with her motionless hand pressed to the totem, staring past them and into the bushes behind.

"I don't like the sound of that," Pauline replied, as gooseflesh traveled up her spine. Nona's playacting was very persuasive. "Is it happening now?" Pauline scanned the area looking for the object of Nona's fixation.

"Not now," Nona replied in a toneless whisper, still staring into the bushes and the mist.

Pauline stepped to the side to investigate between the totem poles and the trees behind them. Craning her neck around, hoping to see what Nona was describing, all she spied was thick bushes, brambles and behind that a wall of trees.

"Who was being killed?" Pauline asked, her voice tight with a hint of curiosity and caution. "I'm impressed you've managed to stand unmoving for this length of time. You're usually fidgeting enough to drive me mad."

Nona remained motionless and didn't respond.

A minute passed before Nona replied, "They've gone now." Her voice didn't waver as she explained, "It was a woman. A young woman. She was being strangled by a man, a large man. I couldn't see his face. I think he had dark hair."

Pauline laughed, but her skepticism made it sound forced. Nona was describing "the tall dark stranger" of every psychic prediction since time began. Now Pauline was sure it was a joke.

"One of those tall dark strangers I should be wary of, is it?" Pauline said sarcastically. "Let's go, Nona. If we're going to walk around Stanley Park before lunch, we can't play games here all day."

Nona, however, continued staring into the trees behind the poles with a trance-like intensity Pauline found hard to bear. She took hold of her friend's arm and pulled her away from the pole.

Nona gasped. She cradled her right hand, as though she was afraid it was injured. She looked at Pauline and said, "I saw a murder. It happened right there." She nodded towards the thick brush.

"Nona," Pauline said, still unsure of her friend's seriousness, "a joke is a joke, but it's gone on too long."

Nona frowned. "I know it sounds crazy, but it isn't a joke."

"If you're serious . . ." Pauline said with a questioning expression.

"I am. This is no joke, Pauline. I wouldn't," Nona replied. "I've never experienced anything quite like that before. Not even the weird goings-on at that house in California were like this!"

"Why don't we look back there," Pauline said, pointing into the bushes.

Nona shuddered. "It was real and yet vague, like shadows in the mist."

"Okay, let's see if these 'shadows' left *footprints*," Pauline said. "But I still think you're teasing me."

"I'm not," Nona protested, as they pushed their way past the branches. They quickly picked up on a trail in the wet grass that led to a stand of trees in the distance.

"Something was here," Pauline said, "maybe an animal, a deer?"

"It's creepy but I know I saw a man strangle a woman," Nona replied.

Pauline studied her friend carefully. She appeared shaken by what she'd seen and not her usual play-acting. "After lunch, maybe we can check the papers or city records and see if there's been a murder in the park that fits what you described. If you're sensitive, it's possible the nature of the totem poles could help you see the history of the place."

Nona shook her head. "It couldn't have been too long ago. They were wearing modern clothes."

"Then it should be even easier to find," Pauline replied. "Recent murders in Stanley Park will be very few, I would imagine."

"What if it's the future?" Nona asked, her shoulders quivering.

"If we don't find a murder in the records, we'll inform the authorities."

"We can't go to the police with a story like this. *You* didn't even believe me, and you were standing right there. I'd be locked up in a mental home for evaluation," Nona replied, with a wry smile.

"Hmm. You have a point there. Maybe we just put it down to lightheadedness and the sea air and say nothing until we're homeward bound."

"We have to investigate," Nona said. "Her body could be lying there in the bushes right now." Nona pointed, and they both turned and stared into the dense tree line.

Pauline and Nona searched the area behind the totem poles.

The only evidence of humans were some tracks in the wet grass, and they could've been made by anyone including themselves.

"There's no one here, Nona," Pauline said gently, as her friend's eyes swept wildly around.

Nona nodded. "Let's walk. The fresh sea air will clear my head." Nona wriggled as if she were trying to shake off a bad dream.

It took some time as they walked around the park's seawall trail, but eventually Nona's spirits were lifted, and by the time they'd chosen a restaurant for lunch, they were back in vacation mode.

"I'll never mock psychics again," Nona said earnestly, as they munched their way through oversized plates of fish and chips.

"It scared me a little just watching you."

"What if we find there was a murder?" Nona asked, dragging a long french fry through a blob of ketchup.

"I say we do nothing," Pauline said. "Nothing in your vision is evidence. We don't want to lead the police on a wild goose chase."

Nona nodded. "And we don't need *another* mystery to spoil *another* trip."

The waitress came to the table to clear the plates, and Pauline asked her, "Have there been any notable crimes in the area as of late?"

The waitress rolled her eyes, shook her head and quickly cleared the table.

Pauline was even more certain her friend had experienced an odd phenomenon but not something the police needed to hear about.

AFTER LUNCH the two friends scanned the papers in the hotel's lobby. No recent murders had taken place in the park. They spoke with the concierge, who confirmed a few old murders, none of which had any resemblance to what Nona had described.

"Puzzling, but not something to concern ourselves with," Nona replied with a shrug.

As they made their way downtown to enjoy some big city life, Nona began to chuckle, and out of nowhere, she commented, "Unless I start reading cards and tea leaves. Then you can get me some proper help."

The women explored the city. All conversation of the incident was put to rest, though Pauline could sense her friend was still shaken. Nona had said this was a unique experience. They'd known each other for some years now and Pauline hadn't picked up on any *sensitivities* in any of their past explorations. The two friends stood waiting for the "walk" signal, when Nona's face crinkled.

"Are you still wrestling with the vision?" Pauline asked.

"I'm trying to recall more of the details, but it's hazy."

"Why don't we head back to the room and relax for the rest of the afternoon. Maybe a good Hallmark movie will shake the grip this has on you."

Nona scoffed, "Neither one of us watches Hallmark movies, and you know it. Although I do appreciate the gesture."

AFTER SPENDING the afternoon relaxing in the hotel, just not with television, Pauline was pleased that her friend had returned to her normal state. An afternoon quilting appeared to have done the trick for Nona. She was no longer staring into space with worried intensity. And Pauline hadn't minded curling up with her classic mystery novel.

However, just as Pauline's novel was wrapping up the clues to its mystery, Nona's efforts were back on the case. "Let's go back to the area and poke around. Can't hurt."

"So much for a quiet evening in, erasing all traces of the day." Pauline shook her head, though she couldn't blame Nona for wanting to investigate. Admittedly, Pauline's mystery novel had revved up her own sleuthing bug. "This morning you looked like you'd seen a ghost. If we hadn't had seafood, I would've said you looked clammy."

Nona groaned, theatrically. "I'm the one who does the bad puns in this duo."

Pauline grinned behind her teacup and sipped gingerly. "I suspect you aren't going to let this go until we do go back, though."

Pauline stood and put her teacup in the sink. "Let's get dressed for the adventure, then."

Nona stopped shifting in her seat, rose to her feet and walked through the suite to her bedroom. " You're right," Nona called back as she entered her room, "I am anxious to put this to rest. Though, I'm not sure if I prefer that we find a body or not."

"I don't like talking to people I can't see," Pauline said, raising her voice.

Nona called out from inside her room, "Can't you hear me through the walls?"

Minutes later, they both came out of their respective rooms, dressed and ready.

Pauline replied to the earlier question, "Oh, I heard you all right. I was just afraid you'd be asking if I can *walk* through walls." They mirrored each other's nervous chuckle, then Pauline asked, "Are you ready to go?"

"Yes, let's take a taxi. So we can get there quickly, rather than walking. My knees are a little stiff after all we've already done today." Nona massaged her knee.

"I really do not understand your fascination with hiring strangers to drive you around," Pauline replied, as she put her windbreaker on.

"What?" Nona replied, shrugging. "You have a problem with taking a taxi? We've taken plenty of taxi rides."

"No. I just prefer to *walk*," Pauline replied. "It's better for me, us, in every way. Do you know how many people are murdered in taxis?"

"Say what? No. Is it a lot?" Nona asked. "Never mind, don't tell me. I overdid it yesterday. We're taking a cab. We can revisit *walking* again tomorrow."

Sighing, mimicking Nona's usual conduct, Pauline allowed herself to be taken on the short ride to Stanley Park's Brockton Point and the totem poles. A short walk all around the poles quickly revealed there was nothing unusual to see. Nothing to suggest a murder had ever been committed or would be likely to be committed. In the late afternoon sunshine, the poles, the trees, and the park were bustling with activity—a picture of normal, everyday life. Pauline decided their special sleuthing talents combined with the suggestion of elemental power in the totem poles had just fired up Nona's vivid imagination.

With relief, in Pauline's case, and disappointment in Nona's, they took another cab to leave the park, this time traveling across the iconic Lions Gate Bridge, which dominated the city skyline. The cab dropped them at the hotel, and they explored from there until it was time to dress for their evening at the opera. As they set out in yet another cab, Pauline smiled, for they were about to enjoy their first vacation sans a murder to investigate.

THE REASSURANCE the two women held the night before was short lived, lasting only until they read the headline the next morning, on the front page of the *Vancouver Sun* newspaper —*Murder Among the Totems*.

"Now what are we going to do?" Nona said, swatting the paper down on the table and pointing to the headline.

Pauline adjusted in her seat and said, with weary resignation, "Now, we investigate." She set her teacup down.

"Okay. But after we finish breakfast, please." Nona grinned.

Pauline picked her teacup up again. "You and your breakfasts. The prime minister himself couldn't drag you away from your scrambled eggs."

Nona forked a mouthful of fluffy eggs and asked, "Do you know the prime minister?" She crunched on some bacon. "Do you think we should tell the police now?"

"I don't. They'll think we're attention-seekers and arrest us just for wasting their time."

"Is that how it works here in Canada?" Nona asked, seriously.

"No, of course not," Pauline replied, with a look of disbelief. Nona heaved a sigh of relief.

"It's an odd story, to be sure. I wouldn't believe it if it hadn't happened to me." Nona gulped down more than half her orange juice.

"And nor will they, or anyone else for that matter," Pauline agreed. "We either walk away, which we never do, or we investigate."

Nona set her napkin over her near empty plate. "We did walk away, that one time, in California."

"Yes, and look how that turned out."

"Embroidered into another murder. Yes, I know." Nona sighed. "The charms of Hollywood."

Pauline sipped her tea, remembering the locked-room mystery that they now called their *California Adventure*. Just another one for the couple of *sassy senior sleuths* they'd turned out to be.

"So we investigate," Nona said again, before finishing the last of her orange juice. "How to even start is the question." She wiped her mouth on the napkin and frowned. "We can't call on regular channels for info, can we?"

Pauline chuckled. "Maybe we should visit a real psychic."

"Silly as that sounds . . ." Nona said, and pursed her lips.

Pauline shook her head. "No!"

"What? It might come to that."

"Let's look at the news to give us some details," Pauline replied.

"That's a funny one."

"This is the early edition of the paper. We need the radio or the TV news for more current, up-to-date reports."

As Nona cleaned her plate, she said, "Well then, what are we doing sitting here? I'm finished. I'll watch the local TV news here while you listen to the radio in your bedroom."

"NOW WE KNOW," Nona commented, after the two sleuths pooled their information. "A young woman was strangled right next to the totem poles in Stanley Park last evening."

She paused, and Pauline glanced up at her. Nona had an

unfamiliar expression, and all Pauline could think to say was, "What is it?"

"I could've warned them of that yesterday morning. Maybe in time to save—"

Pauline cut her off. "We agreed, neither of us wanted you committed." She smiled, and Nona curled her lip in her own half-hearted attempt at a smile. "It isn't much, but it does confirm what you think you saw," Pauline said. "We also know her killer was a large man with curly dark hair based on the eyewitness description given by a jogger in the park, who witnessed the man fleeing the scene."

"We don't actually know that," Nona replied.

"It matches your vision," Pauline replied.

"You *can't* believe in ghosts or premonitions, though, *can* you?" Nona asked.

"It was *your* vision, call it what you will. I do believe there's much more to this world, this universe, than is experienced by our senses, or"—Pauline added emphatically—"by our scientific *sensors*."

"Well, what do *we* know that the police or the reporters don't already know?" Nona asked.

"Not a lot. First we need to visit the crime scene and confirm it is where you envisioned it. This could be just a horrible coincidence. The area 'near the totems' could be anywhere on Brockton Point."

Nona snorted. "Hah! Not likely. They say 'near the totems,' and even if the murder isn't in exactly the right spot, it was there in the vision. I'm sure of it." Nona slung her purse over her shoulder. "And we both know there is no such thing as a coincidence when it comes to investigating murder mysteries." The two women chuckled as they left their suite.

The door clicked closed behind them, and Pauline asked,

"Are you writing a book? You're always worried about coincidences."

NONA AND PAULINE took a short taxi ride back to the totems. The area they'd searched was now taped off by the police, and crowded with press and gawkers—which included the two women, now.

Surveying the chaotic scene, Pauline asked, "What do you want to do about it? We can't just walk around Vancouver hoping to find a man who looks like the one you saw."

"I never suggested that, and it wouldn't help anyhow," Nona said sharply. "He had a raincoat on, and today it's dry and sunny."

"You never mentioned a raincoat. That's something *we* know that the police and press didn't report."

"How will that help us, though?" Nona asked.

Pauline touched her chin with her index finger and contemplated Nona's question. "I don't know if it will."

"Does downtown Vancouver have street artists who sketch or paint? Maybe that would help?" Nona asked.

"I haven't observed any. How about we try to find out anything we can about the girl's family and friends," Pauline began, thinking out loud.

"We don't have the time for that," Nona said. "We're only here for a short while. Besides, how would that go over? Two random strangers just showing up to her family and claiming to have seen a *vision* of her death? Sounds like a kooky television show to me."

"What other options do we have?"

"I think we should look into her love life—a husband, or boyfriend maybe."

"Nothing in the news mentioned a boyfriend. Did more of the vision come through?" Pauline asked with a puzzled look.

Nona put her thumbs to her temples like she was about to receive a cosmic signal. "No, nothing more has been transmitted."

"Oh my word, Nona, really. Where did you pull that thread from?"

They laughed, and Nona replied, "I don't know. My gut, maybe."

WITH NO PLAN, they headed back to their swanky hotel suite. Both women sat on the edge of their seats, watching and listening for more details on the midday news.

From the reports, the two senior sleuths learned the victim had been a happily married woman who everyone loved. And no one could understand how she'd come to be where she was found dead.

"Hah!" Nona squawked, and stood. She paced the room while Pauline sat in the chair, still and calm. "Aren't they always happy and perfect?"

"Sadly," Pauline said, "it often seems that way. People display a public face for everyone, while hiding a very different, private one that only a few ever catch a glimpse of."

"I don't think she was abducted, murdered and dumped there."

"You didn't mention seeing *how* she got there, either," Pauline reminded Nona. "Only what happened *when* she was there."

Nona frowned and then squinted in concentration. "Nope, no signs of how she traveled there or of being abducted." She closed her eyes for another long minute, and her eyeballs danced behind their lids. She opened her eyes. "Her clothes were nice; her hair, makeup were all intact. Like she was dressed up for something."

"Wasn't likely her husband. According to the husband, he was out of town. Maybe she did have a boyfriend after all?" Pauline replied. "You love the scandalous stuff. It would be just like the universe to send you a vision of a scandalous love triangle or something of the sort."

"Maybe," Nona contemplated. "Though, I doubt I'd be that lucky."

"Lucky would be a vacation where there was *no* murder to solve!"

"I think we'd have a better chance at the lottery." Nona laughed, then looked seriously at Pauline. "Do they have a lottery here in Canada?"

"Of course," Pauline groaned, and shook her head.

"Maybe we're letting the press's vivid reconstruction cloud our judgment."

"I never truly believe a word they say." Pauline waved her hand in the air, representing "they." "*So they aren't clouding mine.*"

"Maybe we need to meet her husband," Nona said, snatching up her purse.

"I suspect the husband would be with the police."

"Hmm, okay." She dropped her purse on the table and sat. "According to the police, it most likely happened just after dark. How about we go there tonight? Maybe we'll get lucky, and the murderer will return to the scene of the crime?"

"I think we really have to question how you're categorizing what's lucky and what's not." Pauline chuckled as they both stood, grabbing their purses. Pauline followed Nona. "But I suspect the murderer will show up, because I don't think he's really a murderer."

"Looked pretty murderous to me," Nona huffed, as they walked down the hall to the entrance of the hotel.

"Of course," Pauline said, "it was meant to."

"You think someone's putting on a show in my mind . . . or just in the news?" Nona questioned, but didn't wait for an answer. "Ugh, you have horrible ideas sometimes. How could someone put on a *show* in *my* mind?"

"Honestly, Nona, *my idea.* Don't be dramatic. Just listen to me." Pauline's friend, although dear to her, could be exasperating sometimes. Nona waved to the front desk clerk, and Pauline continued. "I think it's one of those role-playing games, and if we can't get to this man soon, I fear there could be another death."

"Now who's the one being dramatic? Are you having visions now too? Where did you come up with that theory?"

As they stepped onto the bustling sidewalk, Nona replied, "Besides, it serves him right if he does get himself killed."

"Did you call for a cab?" Pauline asked.

"Oh yes, you're going to love this!"

"If it's a clown car, I will not get in, I assure you," Pauline warned, and placed her hands firmly on her hips, giving Nona a pointed look.

"It's not, it's one of those fancy new car-sharing rides!"

"I think you mean ride-sharing cars," Pauline replied, before returning to Nona's earlier comment. "But I don't wish harm on anyone, including the man in your vision." She held up her hand to stop Nona's outraged interjection. "I'm good with people getting the justice they deserve, but it's often the one who initiated the game who becomes the victim in these accidents."

"Role-playing games, clown cars. What's gotten into you, Pauline? Are you feeling okay?"

"I am perfectly fine. Much better than this cockeyed plan to meet a murderer in the woods," Pauline said, as the Modo car pulled up to the curb.

"This is us," Nona told her, as she reached for the door handle.

"Thank you."

DARKNESS FELL as they waited in the park. Nona was fidgeting, and the air was growing cold. A shadowy figure, a man in his early thirties, dressed in a suit, lurked around near the back of the trees. The scene of the crime was still taped off. Pauline nudged Nona. When her friend didn't respond, Pauline turned to look her in the eyes. Nona had once again slipped into a trance-like stare, standing beside the totems.

"It's him," Nona whispered, in an eerie voice. "I'm sure."

They'd hung around for most of the afternoon, watching. There'd been a number of gawkers visiting the scene, eager to share in the vicarious drama of life and death this small part of the park now represented. None could be characterized as viable suspects.

The man in question stopped at the caution tape, his gaze directed at the grass. He stood silently. Soft sobs floated towards the women in the quiet of the evening.

"You go around that way," Nona whispered, gesturing to Pauline to go left.

"I don't . . ." Pauline started, as Nona disappeared in the opposite direction.

They circled the trees and bushes that screened the totems. Not only did the shrubbery provide a realistic backdrop when seen from the front, it provided a perfect screen for their stealthy approach. He was still there, oblivious, when the two women simultaneously rounded the corner and approached him.

Still staring into the empty space before him, he cried out, "I told you you were taking things too far. Why wouldn't you listen to me?"

"I'll listen," Pauline said, surprising the man, causing him to jump back and scan his surroundings. He glanced back and forth between the two women on either side.

He turned to walk away, but Pauline said, "Where are you going? Don't leave. Get it off your chest. You'll have some peace if you do."

Suspects had a way of confessing their truths to her, and she'd been right about their innocence or guilt on many occasions.

"Peace!" He laughed harshly. "I've had no peace since I met her, and I'll have no peace until I join her."

"Nonsense," Nona said. "You're stressed out by what happened, but if it was an accident, you'll still have a life ahead of you."

"An accident? How could it be? She . . . we . . . we had a safe word and a signal." The man grabbed a handful of his hair in despair. "She only had to give me the sign. She knew that."

"But she didn't?" Pauline asked. This wasn't quite what she'd been expecting. When she suggested role-playing earlier, she'd meant folks who hire companies to give them an adventure. Not role-playing of *this* peculiarly *sexual* kind. Pauline was glad she had so little experience with this side of life.

He shook his head. "Every time, it was longer, more danger-ous. I told her we had to stop. I wouldn't do it anymore."

"She wouldn't stop?" Nona asked. She backed up a step, as the man showed increasing desperation.

"She said, 'One more time . . . at the totem poles'. . . She said she wanted to draw in the spirits from all the victims who had been sacrificed to them . . . The perfect moment of ecstasy, she told me. The one she's approached with me, but never quite reached . . . She urged me to do this for her, so she could then return to her ordinary life . . ."

The whites of Nona's eyes showed as they widened in shock.

"But you know these totems are works of art, just for the park," Pauline stated.

"And tourism," Nona added.

"If anyone ever was sacrificed at a totem pole, which I don't believe, surely no one died at *these* ones," Pauline said reassuringly.

He laughed demonically. "I said that to Nikki. It didn't matter to her; the only thing that mattered was she thought she could relate to them somehow. One last time, and then we would stop."

"But it wasn't one more time, was it?" Nona asked.

He shook his head. "We were just getting into it that day when she saw an old woman watching us." He stepped closer to Nona, staring. "It was you?"

Nona nodded. "I saw you. I thought I was seeing things."

"We were both here," Pauline said calmly, pulling his attention back to her.

"We ran," he said. "How we ran. It was almost exciting. We reached those trees over there"—he pointed to a thick stand of firs nearby—"and waited till you'd gone. Nikki couldn't stop laughing all the way home."

"Yet you came back again?" Nona shivered.

He nodded and hung his head. "I said it was over, that we'd done her 'one last time.' She argued we hadn't, because we'd been interrupted. That it had been spoiled before she'd found her 'spirits.'"

The man dropped to his knees and ran his hands through his hair. "We argued, but I could never refuse her anything." He looked Pauline square in the eyes, and his face showed his agony. It was pale and ghost-like. "I didn't understand what she meant."

Pauline understood right away what it meant. "Your 'last time' and her 'last time' were different 'last times'?" she asked.

"I realized the moment she collapsed in my hands. But it was too late." He threw his hands in the air and shrieked, his whole body trembling. "She often told me she could never live without me. I thought it was just a lover's talk. Now I see. When I said 'last time' I meant last time for this terrifying strangling game; she meant it was *the* one last time for the game in her life."

He fell silent, his body slumped and his breath coming in short harsh gasps. Then he continued, "I tried CPR, but I didn't really know what I was doing. She wouldn't respond. So, I panicked and ran."

"You should have called an ambulance and the police," Nona said.

"I couldn't face it. My life would be ruined."

"You must face it now," Pauline replied in a soft, calm voice.

He jumped to his feet and lifted the tape; ducking, he passed under it into the crime scene area.

"I don't have to," he said, and lay on the ground where the grass was already flattened. "When I'm gone, tell them . . . I'm sorry. It wasn't meant to end this way."

Nona was frantically fumbling for her phone. Once in her grip, she began tapping in the number 911. After a moment, she spoke. "We need an ambulance and the police."

As Nona provided details to the operator, Pauline also ducked under the tape and knelt beside the man.

"What have you done?" Pauline asked, her voice trembling with emotion. "Did you take something? You have to stay with us. Help is on the way."

It was already too late—his eyes were rolling back into his

head, and the anguished expression had left his face. His breathing stopped and his expression looked peaceful. Though, Pauline thought, his afterlife would likely be anything but. Or did the afterlife forgive sexual obsession in this one?

THEY GAVE their statements to the police, who accepted their story, which was now more rational than when Nona was thinking it was a vision and more understandable given the context of the man's confession.

"You should have come forward," the inspector scolded Nona. "We might have seen it for what it was and been there to save her. We have experience with these kinds of deaths."

"You wouldn't have believed it. How could you? I didn't believe what I'd seen myself," she replied. "Not really."

"The headlines will read murder-suicide," the inspector huffed. "The press will have a field day."

The two women walked away as soon as the inspector gave them the nod signaling they were free to go.

"Should we speak to the press? They already have a picture of us," Nona asked her friend.

"I think this time, it might be best if we head directly home."

"And we can't really be sure of what happened between them," Nona said, nodding. "After all, we only have his word for it."

"And your vision, as you thought it then," Pauline reminded her. "She wasn't being forced. I think what he said was true. She was actually the suicide."

They walked towards the busy sidewalk. Nona finished Pauline's thought, "And he was the victim."

"She knew he would follow after her death," Pauline continued. "She knew him and knew how her death at his hands would destroy him. *She* murdered *him*, though the law wouldn't say so."

"Not our problem, Pauline. They're both deceased. They can't be hurt by each other anymore."

As they passed a café, Nona commented, "Thankfully, for me, what I saw was an actual observation and not really a vision. But it shows how easily a gloomy day, some towering totems and too much imagination can affect even a super sleuth." She shuddered, brightened and asked, "Shall we eat?"

"I think we should get off our feet."

Nona held the door. "You know, I was beginning to wonder if I was really going to need to get some help. What I saw was real and yet not real, if that makes sense."

"The only help you need, Nona, is with finding our next destination. Preferably somewhere warm, sunny, and filled with happy vacationers. Surely that will wipe away these memories."

10

DANGER IN DEATH VALLEY

CAUTION!
EXTREME
HEAT
DANGER

P.C. JAMES
KATHRYN MYKEL

DANGER IN DEATH VALLEY

Mini Mystery
#10

The descent from higher ground to the bottom of Death Valley made Pauline's ears pop. When she peered out through the windshield, the road was lost in the shimmer of the sweltering heat.

"Looks pretty hot, doesn't it?" Nona wiped her brow even though the car's air-conditioning was keeping the interior at a constant seventy degrees.

"We should stop and step outside," Pauline suggested. "That way we can get the real feel of why it's called Death Valley."

"Let me hit the brakes. I don't want to connect with that soft shoulder too fast," Nona agreed.

Staring through the haze, the two sleuths sat in companionable silence until Pauline cried out, "You said you were going to slow down, not speed up!"

"Oops, wrong pedal."

Nona finally decelerated and parked the car just before a cactus grove. She killed the engine. "I hope the car starts up again. We haven't seen anyone pass by. It would be a long walk if something happened." Nona grinned, showing she wasn't being too serious.

"Why do you always say stuff like that?" Pauline asked, and opened the door. She stepped out, and the heat hit her like a physical blow to the chest. "Wow, I'm glad it isn't any later in the summer."

"It's not a nice place," Nona replied, and lumbered out of the car. She put on her wide-brimmed visor.

Pauline walked around to Nona. "It's beautiful land, but can you imagine crossing this on horseback or in a wagon train of carts and mules?"

Pauline crossed the road and stepped into the sandy wasteland of the desert, heading for a clump of interesting cacti near a rocky outcrop. A quintessential desert scene.

Nona waited, looked both ways and then crossed the road to join her.

"Did you really think a car might pass by?" Pauline chuckled.

Nona shook her head and ignored her friend's quip. "The storm last night has sculpted some amazing dunes." She pointed at the wavelike ridges ahead. "Reminds me of our Nevada trip."

Pauline nodded. The scene was eerie, otherworldly, and oppressive despite the bright sun, tan sand and rocky outcroppings.

"We shouldn't go too far," Nona cautioned, reaching out to grab Pauline's arm. Pauline didn't stop.

"I just want to get a feel for it," Pauline replied. "I want to imagine what it was like for the settlers who first came this way, before there was a road. It's fascinating, don't you think?"

"Fascinating?" Nona scoffed, following closely behind Pauline.

"I hear you rolling your eyes behind my back," Pauline said, not looking back.

"It's madness. Why would anyone cross this way?"

"The rewards outweigh the risks, I suppose. Or did in their minds, anyway. I'm sure they crossed in winter, not like now when we're heading into high summer."

"I'm heading back to the car, Pauline. The heat is getting to me."

"Surely not." Pauline eyed her friend. Nona wasn't joking. Her face was flushed and dripping with sweat.

"You'll have to carry me back to the car if I don't."

Pauline nodded. "Then I think we've learned enough to know how the earliest settlers endured."

Behind Nona, a stark white object was sticking out of the sand at the bottom of a narrow gully. "A bone," she cried, pointing. Pauline made an instant decision that the ground was safe enough to walk on. "You go, I'll join you in just a minute."

Nona hesitated, turned away, and then spun back. "You shouldn't—" But Pauline had already set out, stepping carefully as she walked.

Fearing she would step onto a sand-covered crevice and be swallowed up, Pauline shuddered and stopped. Nona was right. To cross this wasteland in those long-ago days was madness, and it was no different today. She edged forward, testing each patch of ground before putting her weight on it.

At the edge of the narrow gully, she examined the bone and its surroundings. The sun bounced off the hot, shimmering sand, making the bone protruding from the sand at the bottom of the gully appear and vanish before her eyes. The sand looked like exactly what she'd feared. If she stepped down, she could find there was no bottom, just a pit of loose sand that would swallow her whole, as it had this unfortunate creature.

Her curiosity got the better of her. Placing her hat on the

ground, Pauline knelt on it. The sun fried the back of her head and exposed neck, like bacon in a pan, while she brushed the sand away from the bone.

Within minutes she'd dug deep enough to find more remains. "It's a human skeleton." Pauline shivered despite the suffocating heat. The aridity had caused mummification—the remains preserved perfectly with the tattered shirt and pants still in place.

She sat up. Was the skeleton ancient? Pauline examined the area; there was no evidence of recent activity. Her first instinct was that the skeleton belonged to a long-ago settler, but that was little more than her wish not to be involved with another vacation mystery. She wiped the sweat dripping from her brow. Standing, Pauline shook out her hat and returned it to her head.

Looking about, she noted the landmarks that would help them find the spot again. Once she was sure she had the place firmly in her mind she returned to the car, retracing her steps carefully.

When Pauline was back in the car and the door was shut, Nona asked, "What was it? An old wagon wheel?"

Whoever invented air-conditioning will be my hero forever.

Pauline let her body and soul relax in the cool temperature. She shivered again.

"Well, what did you see?" Nona demanded.

Pauline explained the bones. "We need to inform the police or authorities at the first town we come to."

"You're sure they're just old bones?" Nona asked.

"In truth, it could be anyone, from a thousand-year-old Native American to a recent unwary hiker."

Whoever it was, it wasn't a job for the two supersleuths—maybe not even the police. Someone, however, had to be told before the sand swallowed the skeleton again and it was lost.

"Could it be a recent murder victim? We haven't had a lot of excitement on this trip. An investigation would make the vacation more memorable," Nona suggested, grinning.

"I'm sure it would," Pauline replied. "Aren't you the one who always prays for a quiet trip?"

Nona chuckled. "I've seen really old bones. They're usually dry as dust."

"These were mummified."

Nona shrugged and eyed Pauline. "Makes sense they would be, here in the desert."

Pauline recognized the spark of intrigue in her friend's expression. Nona's interest was piqued.

"I say we dig them out to be sure. We might find evidence."

"That's archeology," Pauline said, "not a murder investigation."

"You don't know that." Nona pulled the hat off Pauline's head.

Retrieving her hat, Pauline replaced it firmly on her head and stepped back out of the car. As she did so, a vehicle appeared out of the road haze. She walked to the roadside and flagged it down. Having a witness here right at the start would save a lot of trouble later.

The driver, a slim guy, clearly a tourist—even as pale as they themselves were, and around here pale meant tourist—stepped out of the car and approached. "Do you ladies need assistance? Car trouble?"

"Not car trouble. Body trouble," Nona replied with a grin.

Pauline explained what they'd found.

"You should call the police," the guy said. "The name's Sam, by the way."

Pauline and Nona introduced themselves before Pauline led Sam to the area where she'd seen the bone. Pauline pointed at the gully ahead of them. "Just here, a . . ." she began to say, and then stopped. There was no bone where she was looking. "But I . . ."

Sam surveyed the scene. "What is it you think you saw?"

"Bones. There's likely a whole skeleton in there," Pauline replied, scanning the area before darting to another possible site.

"Ma'am, you need to be careful of the terrain," Sam said, catching and gently supporting Pauline under her arm.

"I know what I saw," Pauline exclaimed, and shook her arm loose.

"Okay, why don't you wait in the car, and I'll take a look around."

Pauline frowned, knowing he was right. She was hot and bothered by the events. Or possibly suffering from the onset of heatstroke. Whichever, she *should* return to the car.

"The bones are not there," Pauline called out to Nona as she approached the car.

The two slipped back into the rental car, and Nona adjusted the vents, blasting all the air-conditioning towards herself.

"I thought you'd marked the spot in your mind," Nona asked.

"I did," Pauline said with utter astonishment.

"And now they're not there?" Nona asked. "You literally just saw them. We didn't move them. Nothing happened. There is no one else here. How can that be?" Nona waved her arm.

"Logically, they should be there," Pauline replied. "But they're not. I wish I'd had my camera with me. Not that it would help today. But it might help the police if the film could be developed quickly."

"Maybe the bones were a mirage?" Nona suggested. "Besides, it might take days for film to be developed in a place like this, and we're not sitting here waiting for that."

"I know the bones weren't a mirage. I touched them. The

roughness of the pitted bones scraped against my hands when I scooped the dirt and rocks away," Pauline whispered.

"I'm sure he'll find them then. Maybe you just missed the spot a bit?"

Nona and Pauline stared out the window for a few minutes.

"Here he comes," Nona said. Nona grasped the door handle, but Sam's head shook, then he rotated his fist in the international gesture for rolling down the window. Nona obligingly lowered the window, and a blast of smothering heat filled the car. She immediately rolled it back up again, opened the door and stepped out.

"Ma'am, there's no need for you to get out of the car. I think you and your friend should head into town and cool off."

"What? What about the bones?" Nona asked.

"I found them. But, give your friend some water . . ."

"Are you saying there's something wrong with her?" Nona interjected before he could finish.

"Not at all. The heat just has her disoriented, so her location was wrong. That's a bad sign in the desert." He waved her off. "When you get to town, phone in what you found. I'll leave a marker, and when I get to my motel, I'll call it in also. Have a nice day, ladies." He patted the roof of their car and walked back to his own vehicle. Nona jumped back into their vehicle, slamming the door behind her.

Pauline knitted her brows, shocked at Sam's implication. "Do *you* think I got it wrong?"

"Well, he sure does!" Nona harrumphed.

"He thinks I'm crazy?"

"Sort of, but it's nonsense. He thinks you have heatstroke, but you're as sharp as a new rotary blade," Nona replied.

Pauline looked up and laughed. "Only you, Nona, would find a way to insert a quilting reference in this situation."

"Well, you are sharp," Nona chuckled. "But," she added seriously, "I think we should get going, and fast. Something isn't right about him. He bothers me. I can't put my finger on it. And no, his problem doesn't have anything to do with your mental acuity." Nona fastened her seat belt.

Pauline did the same. "What exactly did he say?"

"He said he found them but not where you said they were," Nona replied. "He also said we should tell the police what we found when we get to town."

"But *I* looked, and they weren't there. How could that possibly be?" Pauline cried as the car accelerated, spinning its tires in a patch of loose sand. "Hey, slow down, the last thing we need is to be stranded out here."

Nona decelerated slightly as the car shot out onto the road. "He saw them, and he's going to leave a marker. Sounds harmless enough, but like I said, I have a bad feeling."

"All the more reason to not run us off the road," Pauline cautioned. She clutched the armrest.

"What?" Nona asked. "I slowed down." Nona looked in the rearview mirror.

"Can we please think about what has happened here rationally?" Pauline pleaded.

"We shouldn't think about it at all. Let's just get back to the hotel and forget we were ever here." Nona's eyes darted back to the rearview. "Look, Pauline, there are bones, and we should tell the police, like he said. If they're very old, it will be archeological, like you said. In which case, it's none of our concern, and we'll read about it in the paper next week."

"I hope this is not one of your gut musings." Pauline laughed, before adding, "Or that what I'll read in the paper next week is that *you* were the one who found the ancient bones."

"As if I would try to take credit for invisible bones." Nona cackled.

"I'm glad I amuse you, *Ms. Galia*."

"Putting any of this in the news would be bad. I didn't give him our names, *Miss Riddell*, and I don't want the media to do that either. I hope he didn't get our plate number."

"What rattled you so much?"

"I don't know, Pauline. I don't know what it is, but something about that guy is off."

"You just like your men a little more 'rough and tumble.'" Pauline laughed. "Sam is not your type."

"Too young to begin with. But you are right," Nona said, grinning sheepishly. She jolted. "That's it."

"That's what?" Pauline said.

"He wore too much jewelry," Nona said.

"Young people today have a different style of fashion, Nona. Who knows what's in fashion now."

"I still think he was strange," Nona said stubbornly.

"Whether he's strange or not," Pauline replied, "he couldn't have seen the bones when I couldn't find them."

Nona was quiet for a moment. "Like he said, it's easy to get disoriented in the desert. You must have returned to the wrong spot. He looked about and saw them."

"I took careful note of the location and the surroundings," Pauline argued. "Between the devil-horned cactus and the angel's wings boulders."

Nona couldn't contain her laughter. Pauline crossed her arms with an *I'll wait* expression and pursed lips. Nona teased, "All cactuses look like devil horns to me . . ."

"No, most have three arms, not two. Regardless, I knew how hard it would be to find the bones again. I'm sure I returned to the right place."

Still chuckling, Nona suggested, "Could the wind have blown the sand back over them?"

"It could, of course," Pauline said, "but it isn't that windy. We could have done with a breeze to keep us cool, if you recall."

"An animal." Nona's chuckles tapered off. "Burrowing around them and burying them again?" She shot her pointer finger into the air. "Or burrowing *nearby* and throwing the sand *over* them."

"We didn't see any animals; it's the desert." Pauline dismissed the idea and turned her head to gaze out the window as rock formations whizzed by. "How fast are we going?"

"Not too fast." Nona tapped the breaks but the car barely slowed. "There has to be some explanation," Nona continued. "Bones don't appear and disappear . . . as if by magic."

"We have to go back," Pauline said. "We can't leave this unsolved now, even if the bones are ancient."

"No way," Nona replied. "That man wasn't the real deal, and we're not armed."

"We can call the police on your cellular phone and meet them there," Pauline said.

"You know I don't like using those things," Nona grumbled.

"Well, isn't this why you brought it? In case we were out in the wilderness, and we needed help?"

"I guess," Nona agreed reluctantly, "but what can we say? We thought we'd found a skeleton, and when we tried to show the bones to another tourist, they were gone? Then the guy creeped us out, so we left? They're not going to come out here for a story like that."

"Then it's up to us," Pauline said. "We'll photograph what we've found. That way we can prove it, if we must."

"No," Nona protested. "I'm not getting killed for the bones of some toothless old prospector." She clacked her teeth.

Not sure if Nona was proving she had teeth . . . or not, Pauline ignored the disturbance and continued, "If it was a pioneer or prospector, then why would Sam have been so keen to get us out of there?"

"You said the bones were clean and dry, and not a recent death."

"But there are other explanations for the condition of the bones," Pauline said. "Quicklime would explain someone who'd been killed recently."

"Now you're grasping at straws," Nona replied. "And if what you've just said is true, I'm definitely not going back to duke it out with that guy, because if that theory is right, *he* might be the murderer."

"I wish I had my Glock." Pauline scowled. "I never like to travel with it, but that's when I need it the most." She paused. "Particularly when I travel with *you*, Nona."

"Me! How is it my fault?"

"All I'm saying is, when we travel, *things happen*, that's all," Pauline said. "Now, let's get back and solve that mystery."

"And when he sees us again?" Nona asked.

"I'm sure he'll be long gone by the time we get back there."

Nona sighed but slowed the car and swung it around on the empty road. "I hope that Sam guy keeps going south, otherwise he'll spot us."

"Why wouldn't he?" Pauline asked. "Really, Nona, you're obsessing."

"Doesn't anybody live around here?" Nona grumbled. "Apart from that guy, we haven't seen a single vehicle."

"I guess we're not in the height of vacation season here," Pauline replied, as they drove back at a more sedate pace than Nona usually liked to maintain.

Backtracking for what seemed like forever, Pauline carefully watched for anything familiar. "I recognize that rock," Pauline said. "Slow down so we don't miss the crime scene."

"At least Hannibal Lecter has gone," Nona commented, scanning the area.

"He was just concerned about our well-being, Nona,"

Pauline responded. "Two old women parked on an empty road in the middle of Death Valley probably scared him. Maybe he didn't want to have two heatstroke victims on his hands."

"You can make up as many stories as you like, Pauline. He was too nice. You can't trust men who are too nice. It's not natural."

Pauline laughed and shook her head at her friend's strange notions of what was normal and not.

Nona drove past where they had parked, and before Pauline could object, she stopped, backed up and parked near where they'd been less than thirty minutes before.

They looked across the sand and rocks to the outcroppings Pauline had used as her markers. Sam was not on-site, and there was nowhere for him to hide.

"Do you see a marker?" Pauline asked, unlocking her seat belt and opening the car door.

"There's a rock at the roadside," Nona replied, pointing through the windshield, "maybe that's it."

"A rock—in the desert?" Pauline replied. "How is that a marker?"

Nona shrugged.

"It doesn't really matter if there is or isn't; I'm going back to search, and this time, *I'll* leave markers that won't be mistaken."

"I'm coming with you, Pauline."

"You were ready to faint last time," Pauline objected.

"I'm pretty sure it was you who was ready to faint. Besides, I have my hat and a bottle of water," Nona replied. "I'm not staying in the car to be murdered by that guy. We're safer together than separated."

Pauline looked around dramatically. "There's no one here. Not a *living* soul for miles."

They slowly crossed the scorching ground, their energy sapped by the midday sun beating down on them.

"It was this gully." Pauline pointed. "I'm sure of it." She traced the outlines of the devil-horned cactus with her finger. "Which means the bones are under that sand somewhere." She once again knelt on her hat and brushed away the sand with her fingertips.

Nona knelt beside her and prepared to do the same, when Pauline's fingertips hit something solid, and she pulled her hand away. "Ugh."

"What is it?" Nona leaned forward, peering over Pauline's shoulder. Pauline brushed the sand away from a solid belt buckle with an eagle motif.

"I was right," Pauline cheered. "It's a man from the olden days."

"Nah. I've seen buckles like this nowadays. All the souvenir shops sell them. And this doesn't prove it was a *man* either."

"It's badly pitted, and most of the leather's gone," Pauline argued, as she dusted it off. "I'm sure this is an old prospector."

"Then where is he? Or she?"

Pauline sat up; a frown crossed her face as she concentrated. All around, the haze shimmered, making the car hard to distinguish. Had she imagined it? Could a mirage look like a skeleton?

"Sam couldn't have moved the bones," she said at last, "and certainly not this completely. There wasn't time."

"Why was he here anyhow?" Nona asked.

Pauline shrugged and turned to look at the angel's wings rock formation. "He was driving by and stopped to help us." She rose to her feet and walked towards the rocks, scanning the ground as she went.

"Maybe," Nona said, following her. "We should check if there's any more clues in the gully. You didn't see the buckle last time. A tooth would be good. The authorities can get DNA from teeth."

"A tooth in the desert. Not likely. I'd settle for a wallet with credit cards," Pauline said. "You can look for teeth."

"An ancient prospector with credit cards?" Nona questioned absentmindedly. "You know I'm as good for wild theories as the next gal, but I'm beginning to wonder if your vanishing bones might be chalked up to a simple desert animal." She stopped and looked back. "See, the landscape has shifted slightly within the few minutes we just spent here."

As she paced, Nona tilted her head in contemplation. "What might be out here that could have caused the shifting sand? A sinkhole? An animal—oh!"

Nona grabbed Pauline's arm, startling her. "What is it?"

"Back up, Pauline. This way, towards me. Very slowly," Nona urged, waving her free hand for Pauline to come towards her, her eyes bulging wide. "We've found your bones. But you aren't going to like where they are." Nona pointed and screamed, "It's a snake den!"

Nona hustled backwards, nearly taking both women down in her efforts. "Looks like the snakes stole your bones, Pauline."

Pauline peered at the gully, which shimmered in the heat, making it hard to be sure of what she was seeing: a skeletal hand with coppery creatures slithering across and around it.

"Ugh, I hate snakes," Pauline said. "Now it really is a job for someone else."

They cautiously detoured around the gully, which was now alive with snakes. Their thrashing bodies flicked sand back and forth as they twisted around each other in a frenzied macabre dance. Nona and Pauline scrambled back up to the road and out of striking distance. There they took a deep breath before darting to the car. Safely away from the danger, they stopped to marvel at how silly they had been with all their irrational theories. Then they both began to laugh hysterically.

"We forgot to leave a marker," Pauline cried.

Nona laughed. "Maybe that's why Sam left a rock at the roadside and not something recognizable at the gully," Nona suggested.

"It doesn't matter," Pauline said. "I'm not investigating *snakes* —or their victims."

"You're right, we're safe to let the authorities handle this now," Nona stated, wiping the sweat off her forehead. "I'm soaked through." She pulled at the front of her shirt. "Let's jump in the car and get the air-conditioning running."

"You call the authorities with your cellular device right now and get someone down here." Pauline took a long sip from her water bottle. "Finally, we know for certain there really are bones and it wasn't just a mirage."

"I'm not calling anybody till we're well on our way to the motel at Mammoth Lakes," Nona said.

Pauline laughed nervously, but jumped into the car.

Nona drove off the moment they were strapped in, swinging the car around to head north towards the junction that would take them to their motel. She only stopped to call the police when they were miles down the road. Walking back and forth outside as she struggled to find a signal for the phone, Nona suddenly shouted to Pauline, "Hey, we didn't leave a marker."

"We didn't have time," Pauline shouted back through the open window. "And maybe the snakes were why Sam didn't either," she added before winding it firmly shut.

Nona jumped back into the car, snapping the flip phone shut. "Well, what did they say?" Pauline asked.

"They want us to stay with the remains."

"Really? In this heat?" Pauline gaped.

"I guess we need to turn around, again!"

"Fine, though I am staying in the car, in the air-conditioning."

"I think it's best if we both stay in the car," Nona replied.

They parked for a third time near their grisly find. "I think you may be right about Sam," Pauline said. They sat silently for a few minutes as they pondered the events of the day, before Pauline continued, "Him being up to no good, I mean. He said he would leave a marker, but I didn't notice one at the gully. And if he was frightened by the snakes, he could have left one here at the roadside. A rock is just a rock."

"But what kind of 'no good' could he have been up to?" Nona asked. "I'm coming around to your earlier way of thinking, you see. It's likely he was just a coincidence, and maybe he hadn't anything to leave as a marker."

Pauline pursed her lips. "I can't think of any abstract theory to explain it right now, but I do know there is no such thing as a coincidence. That's the only car we've seen today." She shook her head. "What do you think?"

"I think we should be at a hotel, sipping drinks by the pool," Nona quipped.

"What—?" Sirens blared in the distance a cloud of dust behind the convoy. As the dust cleared, Pauline stared mesmerized at the flashing lights from the emergency vehicles racing their way.

Nona grabbed the *oh no* handle above the door. "They're coming in hot. Brace yourself," she said, her head bobbing as she laughed at her own joke. "Why so many?"

They watched as, one by one, four vehicles pulled off and parked on the opposite side of the road.

"The cavalry?" Pauline whispered, and gave Nona a puzzled look.

"What have we stumbled upon this time?" Nona uttered.

MEN SPRANG out of the vehicles. Nona and Pauline watched in bemusement. Nona rolled down her window.

"Ladies," a gangly man in a lab coat greeted them, then asked, "Where are these bones you found?"

The two friends stepped out of the car cautiously and followed the man behind the barricade of emergency vehicles. Pauline pointed to the rocks, but Nona chirped, "It's best we show you. Even we found the area hard to find when we went back."

"Went back?"

"I found them," Pauline explained, "while my friend here, Nona, was cooling off in the car."

"It's hot out here," Nona said defensively.

"At first we couldn't find them again, even though I'd taken careful note of the landmarks," Pauline said.

"Devil's horns and angel's wings," Nona interjected. "And I was just beginning to think she'd been seeing things when we finally found them again."

"Then show us where the remains are," the man demanded, waving for the women to lead him. Several uniformed officers followed the science guy.

"Did someone named Sam call this in as well?" Pauline asked.

The man shook his head. "No. Why?"

"A passerby stopped, and we told him about the bones," Pauline replied. "He said he would."

They led the way towards Pauline's landmarks, both sleuths casting uneasy glances at the ground and each other.

"We should tell you about the snakes," Pauline began, but the man in the lab coat just grinned.

"We know snakes," he said.

"Our footprints have been blown away, and everything looks

different," Nona commented, a perplexed look on her face. She stopped walking and put her hands on her hips.

"Take your time, ladies," a young man in a sheriff's uniform commented. "Deserts are tricky places, and it's easy to get confused."

Pauline detected amusement in his tone, but his earnest expression was genuine. She returned to the search, looking around. Wary of the snakes, she flinched as sand blew over her shoe, her nerves frayed. She sighed in relief when she spotted the area. "Over here."

In a moment, the snake pit was surrounded by police officers staring down at several visible bones and the tattered remnants of the clothes that had once covered the victim's body. The snakes were nowhere to be seen, but Pauline backed up anyway.

"Don't dive in," Nona said. "Last time we were here, this pit was full of snakes."

The officer gave a short laugh. "That's apt, if it's who we think it is."

"Who do you think it is?" Pauline asked. "Do you know who the bones belong to already?"

"A mad scientist who came here a year ago to milk snakes for their venom."

"Why did he need snake venom?" Nona asked.

As the team marked off the edges of the pit with tape and tarpaulin, the man in the lab coat took control of the scene. "For a controversial new drug," he called over his shoulder as he bent to inspect the remains.

By now there was a crowd around the pit, earnestly peering in and ignoring the two sleuths.

"Surely no one in their right mind would let him test snake-oil therapies on people?" Pauline said, to remind them she and Nona were still here. "This isn't the Wild West."

"Or is it?" Nona mumbled, and Pauline silenced her with a stern look.

"He'd done it before, apparently. Found a new drug, I mean," the young sheriff replied, leaving the crowd and walking to their side.

A man in a suit and tie looked up from the pit and spoke to them directly. "Frank Everall was a medical student back in the sixties when he had a single breakthrough and was financially set for life."

"So he was one of your employees?" Nona surmised.

The corporate suit shook his head. "No. We manufactured his original drug under license and were concerned about his later behavior. He could have embarrassed us all, and cost us a fortune, so we've been watching him closely."

The sheriff added, "He arrived in town about a year ago and spent his days wandering the desert, catching rattlesnakes to milk. We were watching him also. He wasn't all there, to be honest."

"And no one knew what happened to him?" Pauline asked incredulously.

"Well, as you can see, ladies, the landscape changes all the time around here." The scientist stood and adjusted his lab coat.

"He's been missing twelve months now." The sheriff gave Pauline and Nona an apologetic look.

"Yet none of you, and no one else, came looking for him in twelve months?" Nona cried.

"Sounds suspicious that he'd just go missing, when so many people were watching him," Pauline said.

"We didn't follow him here," the suit said. "So, to us he just disappeared. We suspected it was for financial reasons."

"Couldn't he have extracted the venom he needed from zoos or other research places? Why did he have to go to such an extreme out here?" Nona asked.

"Frank's been eccentric for some years now," the man in the suit said. "He thought everyone was spying on him."

"Well," Nona said sharply, "he was right, wasn't he?"

"Only to keep him safe," the suit replied.

Nona snorted in disbelief.

The man in the lab coat spoke up and adjusted his glasses. "We don't know if this is the guy, Frank Everall, or his assistant."

"You mean there could be two bodies out here?" Nona asked.

"Could be," the sheriff said, watching the scientist closely. "We only witnessed Frank in town, but then one day a younger man came to the motel in Frank's truck, paid the tab and left. He claimed to be his assistant. Made it a point that they had all the venom they needed and were heading back to their lab."

"And the assistant disappeared too?" Nona asked.

"From what we learned later, evidence pointed to it," the sheriff replied.

"Maybe the assistant murdered Mr. Everall and ran off with the secret formula," Pauline mused. "In which case, there would be only one body."

The officer nodded. "Maybe. We just don't know." He gestured towards the road. "Now, let's get you ladies back to your vehicle. We'll handle things from here. I'll make sure the area is searched thoroughly."

"The bones might be the younger man," Nona suggested, not wavering, and explained about the belt buckle they'd found.

"We must keep an open mind." The sheriff urged the women back towards the road.

"This heat *is* making me a little dizzy," Nona said, as the two women made their way back to the car.

"I'm too old for this," Pauline complained as she plunked into the passenger seat.

"How old are you, anyway?" Nona chirped, starting the engine to get the cabin cool.

"Old enough," Pauline replied as cold air eventually blasted out of the vents, raising gooseflesh on her arms.

"What do you think, Pauline?" Nona asked, breaking the silence. "I think they need our help."

Pauline groaned, flipping the vents towards her. "I say we leave it. Even if it is murder, they have a grasp on the situation. Besides, after a year, if it's criminal, the murderer will have a new identity by now, you can be sure of it."

"If the researcher was murdered for his drug recipe and the venom," Nona stated, putting her hands up to the air vent, "then the assistant might still be found."

"To get involved with the case, we would need the assistant's name at a minimum," Pauline said reluctantly. "The local police will be searching for him now."

"Even if they find his skeleton," Nona said, turning the air-conditioning down, "they have to do some searching anyway. He must have a family who will be looking for him."

"If that were the case, then the search would have begun twelve months ago when he didn't show up to his everyday life." Pauline flipped the knob back to high, and the cool air blew Nona's bangs straight up.

"So, you were right, he's either buried here or he's our murderer," Nona replied.

"Two bodies would be best from our vacation's standpoint," Pauline said despairingly. "We won't let it go now any other way."

"If it comes to that," Nona replied. "They both could have been bitten by snakes, just not in the same place or time."

"Look. Everyone's heading our way again," Pauline said, nodding towards the men approaching the road. "Maybe we can just say our goodbyes and head out."

The sheriff came to the car, and they opened their windows.

"Looks like it's the old guy," he said, "but we need the pathologist to give the official verdict. Where are you two ladies staying if we need to interview you further?"

"We expected to be in Mammoth Lakes tonight," Nona said, "but it's getting late. Is there somewhere in the valley where we can stay the night?"

"We also want to share some theories with you, Sheriff. Is your office nearby?" Pauline asked.

"Tell me now and save time and resources." His demeanor had suddenly turned from empathetic to condescending.

"It would be better to talk in a cooler location," Nona snapped back.

"Fine." The sheriff grinned. "My office, 4 p.m. It's the sheriff's office on Main Street in *Oven Arroyo*, and I'm the sheriff, Matt Struthers. We have a nice motel there too."

THE TWO ELDERLY sleuths were at Struthers's office in good time, where they were greeted by a woman young enough that either one of them could be her grandmother.

Once invited into Struthers's office, Pauline explained who they were and their success assisting authorities in the past. Nona added, by way of a conclusion, "So, you see, we can help, if you'll let us."

His expression suggested he wasn't buying into their story. Nona placed a small traveling scrapbook on his desk, and he thumbed through the newspaper clippings it contained. He closed the book and held silent for a long minute. "Okay, as this doesn't appear to be an actual crime, I guess there's no harm in you helping out."

"Do you think it's just an accident? Where's the assistant? Where's the man's truck?" Nona questioned, and hopped out of her seat. Pauline gestured for her to sit back down. Nona remained standing with her hands gripping the back of the office chair.

"My guess is the assistant died after he went back to join the old man, and his body is out there somewhere," Struthers said. "Possibly when he returned, he couldn't find the old man and died looking for him. The truck had to have been stolen later, when it had sat too long at the roadside. But if we find it is a crime, you ladies will be witnesses."

Nona scoffed, "It was the assistant who killed him and took off in the truck."

"Why? The old man had nothing with him of any value. Would the assistant kill him for the money in his wallet? There's been no activity on his credit cards."

"Can you tell us the timeline of events, Sheriff?" Pauline asked.

"Sure. The old man arrived in town and stayed in the same motel you're in. He spoke to hardly anyone, but he did tell the motel manager why he was here. You can ask her. She's still the manager."

"We will," Nona replied, and edged towards the door.

Pauline ignored Nona's outburst and nodded for the sheriff to continue.

"The guy went out early every morning and arrived back late in the afternoon," he noted, and tapped his pencil on his desk. "Then one day he didn't come back to the motel. And, as I said, a young guy came, saying they were heading home to process what they'd collected."

"Did the researcher actually have an assistant?" Pauline asked.

"Nobody had seen him until then, but he showed up in the truck and knew what the researcher was doing. To someone who didn't know better, and the motel manager didn't, it was all legit. He packed up the researcher's belongings and settled the bill. That was the end of it so far as anyone here knew."

Pauline puzzled over the sheriff's comments for a minute, then asked, "Then how did you know he was missing?"

"Some time ago, Mr. Everall's son called. He hadn't heard from his father in months and had only just learned the old man had come to Death Valley."

"You said his son *called*," Nona said. "Is he local?"

"He's from Massachusetts. He called the motel first, and they put him on to me. We told him exactly what we just told you."

"Why did he decide to inquire about his father's absence after so long?" Pauline asked.

"He was getting married and wanted his father at the wedding," Struthers replied.

"Did he know his father's assistant? Did he call him too?"

"The son wasn't aware of any assistant. Only when his father failed to return contact did he start to get worried. After calling everyone who knew his father, and learning he'd come down here to Death Valley, he started calling hotels and motels."

"We think the assistant murdered him," Nona insisted.

"So you said." The sheriff set his pen down. "But for what and why? He had nothing to gain. We put out a call about the truck when we heard from the son, but it has also disappeared, which is why I said it was stolen. It most likely made it to a wrecker's yard long before we started looking."

"What's the next step, Sheriff?" Pauline asked casually.

"A proper search of the area where you found the remains, and I've called the son to come identify any of the belongings we found with the bones. Failing that, he can give us a DNA sample for confirmation."

"Is he coming here?" Nona asked.

"He'll be flying in tomorrow morning," the sheriff replied.

"He's eager to have his father's disappearance settled quickly. Then we'll wrap this up."

"Eager? Disappearance settled quickly? Why?" Nona scoffed, and squeezed the back of the chair until her knuckles turned white.

"I told you, he's now married and wants this puzzle solved," Struthers said. "I think he's after the inheritance but that's just the cynic in me."

Pauline eyed Nona and asked, "And the assistant?"

"My guess, he's dead. Death Valley is an unforgiving place for those not familiar with it. Either we'll find him with our search tomorrow or he'll *turn up* later on, the same way the researcher did. It's just a matter of time."

"He's not a root vegetable," Nona said indignantly.

Pauline stifled a laugh behind tight lips, and the sheriff stood. "I'll walk you out now, ladies."

Pauline stood, taking his cue that the meeting was over, but Nona wouldn't let it go. "So you surmise two experienced men were accidentally bitten by snakes?" Nona asked sarcastically. She followed Pauline out, saying, "I can understand one, but not two."

As Struthers ushered them to the exit, he shut the conversation down. "We don't know they were both *experienced*. The researcher could have stepped into that snake pit and died almost instantly, and the assistant could have gone for help but became disoriented like you did and was himself bitten, only not nearby. Or it could be the other way around. The assistant was bitten farther out, and the old man, hurrying back to his truck to get help, stumbled into that pit."

As Pauline and Nona made their way back to their motel room, Nona said, "Do you buy any of this?"

"Not entirely," Pauline said, "but Struthers said the man's credit cards haven't been used, and, so far as I know, no one has announced a breakthrough therapy using snake venom. The sheriff might well be right."

"I wish we had a name for that assistant," Nona said. "Then we could follow up with a background check or with his relatives."

"Yes," Pauline said. "Why hasn't the assistant's family been in touch?"

"Maybe he's an orphan." Nona shrugged.

"What if it was the son?" Pauline cried. "He comes here a year ago, murders his father, pretends to be the assistant, dumps the car and returns home to wait for his father to be declared missing and then dead. He's getting married and, Struthers is right, wants his father's estate, including those royalty payments from the old drug. He benefits from this death, it has to be him."

"But he called the authorities, and he'd be taking a terrible risk in returning here," Nona replied. "The motel manager might recognize him or even his voice."

"Appearances and voices can be changed."

"Appearances, yes. Voices not so easily. We must get the motel manager and the son together tomorrow and see what happens."

IT WAS clear to the mature sleuths that the sheriff had the same idea. They were summoned to the sheriff's office the next day, and, when they arrived, Juanita, their motel manager, was there along with a stranger the sheriff introduced as the researcher's son.

"Mr. Everall," the sheriff said to the man, "I thought you may want to talk to Juanita. She was the only one, that we know of, who talked with your father enough to be useful. She might be able to shed some light; maybe enough so you can help us understand what happened."

Everall nodded. "That's good of you, Sheriff. Though I'm not sure how I can help."

"Can you speak to his history, or what he was trying to accomplish out here?" Struthers asked.

"He discovered a drug back in the day, but you need to understand, he tested it, and many others, on himself," Everall replied. "He had a mental breakdown. When he recovered, he became reclusive. Cut off all contact with my mother and me."

Prompted by the sheriff, Everall viewed the fragments of cloth, leather, and the belt buckle before shaking his head. "Truth is, Sheriff, while I'd spoken to my father fairly regularly, I hadn't actually seen him in years. I wouldn't know if these were his or not."

"Then we'll need to get a DNA sample. Do you have any reservations about that?" the sheriff asked.

"None at all, Sheriff. I lost my mom three months ago to cancer, and if this *is* my dad, I've lost him too." Everall's eyes glazed over, and he added, "I must know."

Nona turned in her seat towards Everall and asked. "Do you know if your father left a will?"

"I don't know, it's unlikely."

"Then you may be a very rich man," Pauline commented.

Everall's face flushed. "That's not why I'm here."

"Of course not," Pauline said. "I wasn't insinuating that. It was simply an observation."

Everall didn't respond, but his expression remained angry right through the DNA swabbing routine. The sheriff's brows were knitted, but he said nothing, only asking Juanita to tell Mr. Everall about his father's last days.

As Juanita spoke, Pauline kept a steady watch on Everall *and* Juanita. Neither showed any sign of recognition of each other.

Everall was bearded today and could have been clean-shaven a year ago, but his voice didn't sound forced or unusual in any way. She was certain he wasn't putting on an accent or any other device to disguise its sound. She didn't pick up any signs pointing to Everall being the assistant who'd appeared from nowhere and disappeared again.

"Juanita," Pauline said. "Did the man who came to settle the researcher's bill have an accent? Was he from around here or not?"

"Not from around here," Juanita said. "From the East Coast, like Mr. Everall."

"But not Mr. Everall?" Nona asked.

"No. The man was much thinner, shorter, clean-shaven, and blond," Juanita said, shaking her head. "Not in appearance like Mr. Everall at all."

Nona glared at Everall's red head, and Pauline was sure Nona wasn't convinced. The coy look on Nona's face meant one of her wild theories was brewing, or she was cooking up fancy dinner plans.

Everall eyed the two sleuths ferociously, which also puzzled Pauline. Surely their questions were a benefit to him.

When the sheriff was done with the DNA test and the swab was sealed in its vial, Struthers said, "I have some paperwork for you to sign, Mr. Everall, but, ladies, you're free to go. Thank you for your help, Juanita."

Pauline and Nona left the office with Juanita following them.

"Can you tell us anything more about the man who paid Frank Everall's bill?" Nona asked.

Juanita shrugged. "He was just a man."

"Have you seen him since?"

Juanita shook her head, and a few tendrils of hair loosened from her braid. "Not before or since."

"You said an East Coast accent," Pauline said, "but were his clothes local?"

Juanita frowned and straightened her suit jacket. "His clothes were city clothes, and he wasn't suntanned."

BACK AT THE MOTEL, once Juanita was out of earshot, Nona asked, "What are you thinking?"

"For dinner or the case?"

"The case, Pauline. We already have reservations."

"The person who magically appeared yesterday, Sam, was short and thin." Pauline scanned her key card and opened the door when the green light flashed. Nona followed her into the room, tossing her messenger bag on the chair by the door. Pauline continued, "And his hair was blond. Is Sam the assistant, from a year ago?"

Nona retrieved two cold waters from the mini fridge and handed one to Pauline. "No one would just hang around the road waiting to waylay people who stop just there, would they?" she asked.

"But what if they needed that inheritance now and he'd come to move the body? To make it more discoverable, I mean? Maybe waiting another nine years so they could declare the old man dead was too long?"

"On the very day we stopped?" Nona asked. "I know we're often in the right place at the wrong time for evildoers, but that would be a huge coincidence."

"We need to know if there's some reason Everall needed the money now. Or, failing that, if he's applied to have his father declared dead. That would help us be sure of his motive—the inheritance."

"But what has that to do with Sam?" Nona asked.

Pauline's brow creased as she deliberated. "Something about this case doesn't ring of truth. Sam must be Everall's cohort."

"You amaze me sometimes," Nona teased. "I didn't like the guy but I'm not actually dreaming up ways to make him a murderer."

"It's in the hands of the police, now, and if I'm right, it has *everything* to do with Sam," Pauline replied.

"I'm not following, is that code?" Nona slumped onto the couch.

"What time is our dinner reservation? We need to call Struthers again—and quickly," Pauline replied.

THE NEXT EVENING when Struthers called to say they'd made the arrest based on Pauline's theory, he asked, "How did you know?"

"Nona thought Sam was a strange guy," Pauline said, on the speakerphone at the motel in Mammoth Lakes, the women having already made it to their next stop after Death Valley. The cool mountain air was a relief after the desert's furnace-like environment. "Nona couldn't quite place what it was, but she put me on the track when she said 'too much jewelry.'"

Struthers nodded. "It was bad luck for the culprits that you two arrived there when you did. And sensing something wasn't right as well."

"We have keen senses, tuned to catch things others miss," Nona said. "I admit, though, I didn't catch on right away."

"It was the wedding bands," Pauline explained, sensing Struthers was still puzzled.

"Wedding bands?" he asked.

"A fashion statement maybe, but not likely for a *man* in his forties," Pauline replied.

"Sam was wearing a small diamond *engagement* ring," Nona added.

Pauline cleared her throat. "*I* chewed on that, like a bone"— she smirked—"thinking, why would a *man* wear two rings, including a diamond, on the same finger?"

"Hey, *I* knew there was something wrong with him from the get-go!" Nona pointed out. With a grin, she added, "I just couldn't put my *finger* on it. If you'll pardon the pun."

"Quick-thinking criminals," Struthers said, ignoring Nona's quip. "Sam—Everall's wife—Samantha, flew in a few days ago, and their plan was for Samantha to pose as a man and phone in the discovery, but they realized that having you report the bones would be even better. By the time Everall's son phoned us, the bones would have been found, and he could fly in and verify them."

"The bad luck for them was that we saw Sam, I mean Samantha, in the desert—at all really. If we hadn't, no one would've been the wiser," Nona said.

"Yeah, that was a blow to their plan," Struthers replied. "Still, any other passerby might not have thought anything of it, and the criminals still would have been okay. Mr. Everall started the process for declaring his father dead a few weeks ago. We dug into his finances and found that he had significant debts. Samantha caved and confessed, she was to uncover the remains and call the police from afar, directing them where to find the body. They banked on no one ever seeing either of them. With you finding the body, though, they had no choice, except tell you to call the police and bring us to the remains."

"They must've known enough about bodies, or the harsh desert conditions, to know he'd be just bones by now," Nona said.

"They're both in the field of medicine," Struthers said. "Their plan was a good one. Your assistants theory was good. Would've made the perfect cover. If they'd known you were there, then the wife wouldn't have needed to get involved at all."

"From now on," Pauline said firmly, "I'm never leaving the beaten path. Everywhere we go, we find a body. We haven't had an actual vacation yet."

"Will they be charged with murder?" Nona asked. "Because we're sure it was."

"That's above my pay grade," Struthers replied. "They claim they found him dead in his car sometime last year and they panicked, burying his body in that gully, thinking no one would believe them. Thinking we'd assume the worst—that they killed the old man for the inheritance."

"Well, they did," Pauline objected.

Struthers laughed. "We could never prove that but we've charged them with abusing a corpse, but that's likely as far as it will go."

"I hope justice is carried out," Pauline added. "Horrible way to treat his own father."

"Put it out of your mind, ladies. Enjoy the rest of your vacation," Struthers said. "The world goes on every day with much worse than that."

Nona laughed. "Don't we know it!"

SASSY SENIOR SLEUTHS MYSTERIES

11

SILENCED IN SUDBURY

PART 1

CAFE

COFFEE

POLICE LINE DO NOT CROSS

P.C. JAMES

KATHRYN MYKEL

SILENCED IN SUDBURY PART 1

Mini Mystery
#11

Pauline

Pauline adjusted in her own seat as Nona asked for the umpteenth time, "Are we there yet?"

Pauline scowled as Nona's knees pushed insistently into her back. As Nona shifted impatiently in the backseat of the limo they'd hired to take them from Toronto to Sudbury. Their destination—Science North, the famous science museum, with the added bonus of Canada's lush northern landscape.

"Shall we switch places? Then you can sit in the front seat and see we're not there yet," Pauline replied, peering over her shoulder at her friend. "You are sixty years too old to be squirming in your seat like a five-year-old."

Nona tsked. "We've been driving for hours."

"According to this TimTim"—Pauline leaned forward and squinted at the small talking box—"we have forty-three minutes to go. Can you possibly make it that long?"

Nona was silent, and still, for about ten seconds before squirming. "I can't."

Pauline and the chauffeur exchanged glances of annoyance.

"And it's called a TomTom," Nona huffed. "Pauline, we have to stop at the nearest rest area so I can stretch and relieve myself."

"You've stretched and relieved yourself three times since Orilla. Surely you can manage," Pauline urged, turning her head and staring Nona straight in the eyes. "This was only supposed to be a three-hour ride to Greater Sudbury."

Studying Pauline, and then eyeing Nona in the rearview mirror, the chauffeur said, "Ma'am, we have already passed Albin. We won't find a place until we get closer to our destination. It's about a half hour to go now. Or would you like me to pull over to the side of the road?"

Nona scoffed and made a few more disgruntled noises before settling.

Ten minutes passed, and Nona spoke up. "I don't know why you had to sit in the front seat, Pauline. It's weird."

"I told you, I couldn't stand your fidgeting. It was like I was sitting next to a hot potato."

Nona chuckled. "This trip had better be good!"

"What are you going on about now?" Pauline asked.

"Nothing, just please hurry!"

Another ten minutes later, they approached a small town. "Here we are. Signs of life, ma'am," the chauffeur said with an appreciative tone. "There is a Jim Thorntons up ahead, will that do for you, ma'am?"

"Yes, yes, pull in. Pa-lease!"

The chauffeur turned into a parking spot at the popular Canadian coffee shop. The door handle snapped repeatedly as Nona tried to open the door.

Pauline turned her head to face Nona in the backseat. "At least wait until the engine is turned off, Nona. What's the hurry?"

The driver put the town car in park, turned off the ignition and jumped out of the vehicle.

"It's the new medicine I'm taking, I'm sorry." Nona grimaced, and then she squealed, "Let me out!"

She still had her hand on the handle as the door jerked open, nearly causing her to topple out. She caught herself and scurried away.

Pauline pressed the window control, and the glass silently disappeared. She eyed Nona, who was not so gracefully making a mad dash for the coffee shop's entrance. Pauline turned and shrugged, giving the driver an apologetic smile.

Minutes later, Nona emerged with a tray of three cups and a bulky paper food bag.

Pauline stuck her head out the window and called to Nona as she approached, "Do you think you should be drinking coffee right now?"

"We're going to need refreshments, looks like we'll be here a while."

"And why is that?"

"I had to climb over a body to get to the toilet." Nona shrugged one shoulder and her straight bob twitched but maintained its perfect shape. "Now we have to wait until the police arrive."

Nona

Nona was glaring out the side window at the trees flashing past, wondering which one would make a suitable relief station.

It's not my fault I have to pee so bad my back teeth are floating!

The driver of their hired town car kept looking back at her in the rearview mirror and smiling, like he was enjoying watching her squirm.

Couldn't we get a driver with all his teeth? He's probably one of those hockey players; they are always missing front teeth. Nona stifled a chuckle.

A whine escaped her lips as the driver pulled into a parking spot at a popular Canadian coffee shop.

Oh thank goodness, there's Jim Thorntons.

She grabbed the door handle and pulled repeatedly.

Dang child-safety locks, let me out!

"At least wait until the engine is turned off, Nona. Where's the fire?" Pauline asked her as if she didn't already know.

"It's the new medicine that I'm taking, I'm sorry." Nona grimaced, and then squealed, "Let me out!"

The door opened. Nona nearly fell to the ground.

I swear he did that on purpose.

She scrambled to her feet and made a run for the coffee shop.

Oh my goodness, I'm not going to make it!

She did a little dance as she grabbed the door handle. Nona spun her head around, looking wildly for the bathroom sign, and as soon as she spotted it, she ran like she was being chased. As she reached for the doorknob to the ladies' room, an unnatural redhead in a bright yellow dress pushed the door open and bumped into Nona as she was exiting.

"Excuse me, I've gotta go!" Nona said, looking into the woman's bright blue eyes.

Oh, thank heavens!

What? No way, not a body!

I can't stop.

I can't stop, I'll never make it! Sorry.

A MINUTE LATER, Nona was relieved, had washed her hands and was leaning over the body that was sprawled across the bathroom floor. A trail of toilet paper stuck to the woman's foot, leading towards the bathroom stall.

Warm. Hmm.

She touched the victim's wrist.

No pulse. Hmm. The redhead!

She peered out from the bathroom door and eyed the exit sign over the back door.

She probably made a quick escape out the back?

Nona took a few steps and reached her hand out to the exit door, but hesitated.

I hope this doesn't set off an alarm before I have a chance to report the crime.

When she pushed on the crash bar, the door latch clicked and the door opened with a screeching alarm. She scanned the parking lot. The area was clear: no cars, nothing out back but the dumpsters.

I better report this before someone else stumbles on the crime scene and contaminates the evidence.

Walking up to the counter, Nona ordered, "I'll have three

coffees and two orders of Tater Tots, please. Also you're going to need to call the local police, there's a dead woman in the ladies' room." She scanned the room and saw the redheaded woman sitting at a table with a bearded man. Neither of them looked friendly.

The young server raised his eyebrows, but ignored Nona's request and entered her order. "Will that complete your order, ma'am?"

He stared at her with a smile, the fluorescent lights gleaming off his braces.

"Nope, that's it. Just my order and 911 or whatever the Canadian version of emergency services is here."

"Are you joking?" His expression changed from the customer-service smile to a look of panic.

"No, of course I'm not joking."

The kid turned to pick up Nona's order, organized it on a tray and then placed the tray on the counter. "Here's your order. I-I-I guess I'll call my manager."

"You should probably call the police or 911." Nona leaned closer to the kid. "I believe the killer is still in the building." She nodded her head and raised her eyebrows. "I'll be waiting out front. I'm a witness, but I'm famished and my friend is waiting for me to return."

Nona grabbed the coffee tray and food bag and exited the front door, then made her way back across the parking lot to the car.

Pauline rolled down her window and asked, "Do you think you should be drinking coffee right now?"

"We're going to need refreshments, looks like we'll be here a while."

"And why is that?"

"I had to climb over a body to get to the toilet," Nona replied. "Now we have to wait until the police arrive."

.   .   .

Pauline

"Sᴀʏ ᴡʜᴀᴛ?" Pauline asked, hardly able to believe this was happening again, but hesitant just in case this was just Nona's idea of a bad joke.

"Is your hearing faltering?" Nona asked, handing out a coffee and packet of Tater Tots to Pauline and a coffee to the chauffeur as if she hadn't just dropped a sack of potatoes.

"My hearing is just fine. Is this real, or are you just winding me up?"

"It's real," Nona replied, before taking a sip of her coffee. "She, the victim—I mean, the body, of course—was lying half on the floor and half leaning against the wall." Nona sipped again. "The body was still warm. The culprit must've been the woman I bumped into who was leaving the washroom as I entered."

"What's all over your sleeve?" Pauline asked, eyeing a smudge across the sleeve of Nona's perfectly paired outfit.

"I don't know." Nona dipped her head. "I don't see anything. Maybe I spilled my coffee?" Nona swiped at her shoulder, completely missing the blotch altogether.

"Never mind. Where is she now? The murderer, I mean?"

"Still inside," Nona replied. "We can stop her if she tries to leave before the police arrive." Nona shrugged. "This coffee is good, but way too hot."

"How do you know she was warm? And dead? And something nefarious happened?" the driver asked out of turn.

"I checked, of course. For a pulse," Nona replied, wiggling her eyebrows before removing the lid of her cup and blowing on the coffee. "It's always murder!"

"How do you know she's not going to exit out the back of the building?" Pauline asked.

"Her car has to be out front here somewhere. Anyhow, we'd hear the alarm." Nona looked around the parking lot. A dozen cars were parked in clusters. "There's nothing out back except forest. I checked before I ordered." Nona put the lid back on the coffee. She balanced the cup in her palm while holding the food bag and pulled a couple Tater Tots out and popped them into her mouth. "Too crunchy," she said, chomping down on them.

A police cruiser pulled into the parking lot, siren blaring and blue and red lamps flashing. Stopping abruptly at the entrance of the coffee shop, the alarming screech ended.

Nona set her coffee and food bag down on the hood of the car and strolled up to the police officer, who was exiting his vehicle.

"I found the body," Nona said, loud enough that Pauline could hear her though she was still sitting in the town car with the window rolled down. If this was just a case of Nona giving a witness statement and them all leaving, they could still reach their hotel in Sudbury by evening, but she knew Nona too well. Nona would not let this go now that she was so central to the murder.

The policeman, however, didn't seem as impressed with Nona's declaration as Nona had expected him to be, as he stood scowling at her, his posture ramrod straight.

Nona

NONA SPOKE LOUDLY, for Pauline's sake. "Officer, I am a witness. I'm prepared to give you my statement. My friend and I can assist you with the investigation. It's what we do."

He didn't flinch; his expression remained solid. "Wait here, madam. We'll get to witness statements after we've looked at the scene and when additional help arrives." He left her standing there and marched off into the coffee shop.

"Well"—Nona said, returning to and leaning against the town car—"there's gratitude for ya. I could have told him everything he needed to know to make a successful arrest and be the hero of his local force. Maybe I'll have a senior moment and forget what I saw." She crossed her arms and grabbed her now cold coffee. To show them who's boss, she took an aggressive gulp, then choked.

"We can tell them what we know and leave them to get on with it," Pauline said. "We aren't here to solve local murders. It'll probably turn out to be some sordid local gang or adultery affair." Pauline paused. "Not our style and not our concern, Nona."

"Gangs in Sudbury, Pauline? I think you're losing it!"

"I'm not losing anything—not my hearing, not my sense. You, on the other hand . . ."

"But the killer has to be the woman I saw," Nona said, getting back into the car. "The case is as good as solved. The police just don't know yet. But I do."

"When you explain, they'll know it, and we can continue our trip to the *Science North* museum," Pauline replied. "That is why we are here, remember? Well, that and the empty north, the Canadian Shield, the wilderness, the lakes, the escape from civilization . . . escape from people."

"And how does a museum fit into that escape from civilization?" Nona asked. "Look, my showing them the answer will take ten minutes. And all the wonders of nature will still be there when I'm finished."

Pauline groaned. "There's always a setback or a barrier that sends us off chasing our tails for hours, or days."

Additional police cars arrived and then an ambulance. Their

occupants hurried inside the coffee shop, leaving Nona even more fidgety than she'd been on the drive up.

Sitting in the car, the three watched the scene unfold, Nona crumpled her food bag absent-mindedly.

"The victim was probably a Bruins fan," Nona mumbled from the backseat.

"Are you insinuating that a Canadian would murder someone for their choice of sports team?"

"I would have murdered someone for a bathroom not twenty minutes earlier," Nona replied with a chuckle.

"That's not funny." Pauline gave an apologetic smile to the driver.

"Pff. Finally," Nona muttered, as the original policeman, followed by a suited professional, exited the building and headed towards them.

"Good. Now tell them what and who you saw, and we can get on with our trip."

Walking up to the car, the police officer spoke in a commanding tone. "Would you please come with us," he said to Nona, gesturing towards the coffee shop.

"Of course," Nona said, stepping out of the vehicle. "I know who your culprit is. I can easily identify her. I saw the woman leaving the washroom. I've burned her image into my mind." Nona followed the officer and the suited female detective to the front of the coffee shop.

"Finally," Nona muttered to herself, and checked her watch.

It's been thirty minutes!

If I can give him my statement quickly, we can get out of here and still reach the hotel in Sudbury by evening.

He stayed one pace ahead of her.

This policeman doesn't seem very impressed.

I hope Pauline won't be too disappointed that I landed us in the middle of another investigation.

He strode into the restaurant, and Nona followed.

I don't know what Pauline was prattling on about gangs and adultery. Usually, I come up with the fanciful theories. How can she be thinking about museums at a time like this?

Wrapped up in her own musings, Nona was only half paying attention to the crowd inside the coffee shop. The scene had changed. The customers had been corralled in the seating area, and the staff was huddled behind the serving counter. The officers were scattered about, jotting down witness statements on small notepads. The smell of coffee in the air was stale, and all eyes were suddenly trained on her.

"That's her," the unnatural redhead shouted from beside a countertop coffee bar. Her finger pointed directly on Nona. "She's the murderer. The one I told you about."

What?

Nona's sense of pride was instantly replaced with fear. She was being singled out as a murderer, in a foreign country. "Now wait just a minute." Nona raised her own hand and pointed back. "She's the murderer. She's the woman who *I* saw leaving the washroom as I entered it. Details you would have known right at the start, if you'd taken the time to listen to me."

"Have a seat, madam," the officer said, taking her by the upper arm and guiding her to a table with only two chairs. "I'll take your statement now, and maybe we can decide which of you is telling the truth."

Nona bit her tongue, but she couldn't relax her jaw muscles. Her hands clenched in a ball.

Breathe. The officers don't know yet how the events really unfolded.

She answered his questions: name, her address in the States, why she was in Canada. He wrote down the details and then handed his notepad to the suit.

"I'll check her story out, Clive," the female suit replied.

"You'll find everything I've told you is true," Nona snarled.

Clive smiled. "I'm sure we will, ma'am. Now, what can you tell me about what you saw here before you reported the murder?"

"We stopped here so I could use the bathroom. I'm taking a new medicine that is causing me to have to . . . go . . . frequently. I reached for the door when that woman"—she pointed to the redhead again—"nearly knocked me over. I'm an elderly woman, you see." She paused and waited for the officer, Clive, to acknowledge her comment. When his eyes glazed over, she continued. "I would've reported the body sooner, but then we'd be dealing with an entirely different *mess* right now." Nona raised her brows in mockery, then continued. "After I washed up, I checked the body for signs of life. At the moment, I'd forgotten about the redheaded suspect—you know, because of the dead body and all."

"Then you asked the staff to call the police?" He nodded towards the cashier who'd taken her order earlier.

"Well, I also checked the back door. I don't really know what made me think to do that. Hindsight, I realized the woman hadn't actually left the building. I know because I spotted her while I was placing my order. In my professional opinion, the dead woman died trying to get to the door."

"And what kind of professional are you to make that assumption?" Officer Clive asked.

"Again, you would know this if you had taken the time to hear me out when you arrived."

He gave her a stern look, and she continued.

"I am an amateur detective. Or a mature sleuth, if you prefer." Nona quirked a grin, which was quickly replaced by pursed lips when the officer made his stern look more ominous.

"Secondly, it's not an *assumption.*" Nona crossed her arms. "It's the truth, evidenced by the trail of toilet paper stuck to the victim's shoe, which led right to the other stall." She raised an eyebrow, sizing up her opponent.

See, I know what I'm doing. Yes, I did some investigating of my own, young man!

"Let me review the statement given by the woman who is accusing *you*." He pulled out another small spiral pad from his shirt pocket and glanced at his notes before speaking. ". . . It says the deceased, Miss Travis Tee, is her friend. They went to the privy together. The deceased stayed to fix her makeup while Ms. Scarlette Ruddy lined up to place their order. She claims her friend was very much alive when Scarlette left the washroom."

"Her name was Travesty?"

The cross look on his face faltered for a split second.

"Look, Officer," Nona said, giving him an even sterner *I am your elder* look. "With all due respect, this is a farce. I don't even live in this country. I've never been to this location before in my life. We wouldn't even have stopped here if not for my blasted medication. Why would I randomly kill someone I've never met? I'm an elderly woman, for heaven's sake!"

"I'm sure we'll uncover the reason, Ms. Galia," the officer replied, directing a pointed look over Nona's shoulder.

The female in the pantsuit walked up to the table, and Officer Clive smiled. "Ah, here's the detective now. Did you get the confirmation we need so Ms. Galia can be on her way?"

"Actually . . ." She signaled for the interrogating officer to stand up and have a side chat. He stepped out of earshot of Nona.

Nona stared at the two, trying to understand their expressions. She couldn't even read their lips, but shocked, horrified and appalled were the words that came to her mind regarding their expressions.

This makes no sense.

The two officers whispered, then they both looked squarely

at Nona as if deciding on a desperate course of action. The woman signaled another male officer to join them for more whispered discussion.

Well, this can't be good.

Officer Clive returned to the table. "Would you come with us for a moment? There are some additional questions we need you to answer."

Oh boy! Here we go.

Nona rose and reluctantly followed him. He stopped abruptly and took his handcuffs from his belt. "I hope you won't make any trouble, Ms. Galia. The situation would be best for everyone if you remain calm." He nodded to the other male officer who, Nona could now see, had his gun trained on her midriff.

Her eyes bulged. "What's going on . . . ?" Before she could finish her statement, the clanging of metal cuffs caught her attention, and her hands were shackled by the cuffs.

"I'm sure you know," Clive replied. "Now, let's go."

What the heck is going on here?

Nona struggled against the officer's grip, and he tightened his hand around her arm.

"It seems your government is anxious to have you back. Quite a list of crimes you have to answer for."

"There's been some mistake . . ." Nona started, but neither man was listening.

Nona allowed them to lead her out of the coffee shop to the parking lot. Even from across the parking lot, the alarm on Pauline's face was evident.

Pauline

The minutes had been ticking slowly after Pauline eyed her friend walking back into the building. She'd no sooner stepped out of the car to stretch her legs with a short walk than the officer headed towards Pauline and the chauffeur. Pauline rushed across to meet him, while additional police came out and formed a wall between her and Nona.

"What's the meaning of this?" Pauline demanded.

"This woman has been identified as the one seen leaving the washroom where the body was found," the officer replied. "We must ask you and the driver to follow us to the station. These two officers will ride with you."

"My friend and I solve murders that others can't." Nona guffawed. "And we'll solve this one too. Pauline will show that woman for the murderer she is."

"That's unlikely. The woman you're accusing of murder is an undercover police officer."

"That doesn't make her innocent," Nona replied. "It has to be her. There was no one else around."

"Which is why the suspect has to be *you*," Clive replied, putting Nona into the backseat of his cruiser. He fastened a seat belt around her, all hints of a delightful vacation closed off by the slamming of the car door.

Pauline walked back to the car to explain the situation and ask the driver to get back in the car. They both slid into the town car and buckled themselves in. The click of the seat belts echoed through Pauline's ears like the clanking of a jail cell door, and Pauline started hyperventilating.

The chauffeur whispered, "Deep breaths, ma'am. I'm sure everything will be fine." The two officers climbed into the back-seat and fastened their own seat belts, sending a new wave of panic through her. In all the cases they'd come upon during their travels, their involvement had never become this precarious.

"Fine? Fine is a four-letter word," she replied, a little too loudly. She didn't want the police officers to know she was rattled. "My American friend getting arrested on Canadian soil is anything but fine!" This time she hissed the words at the driver.

Her next words she spoke loud enough for the two officers in the backseat to hear her. "Well, sirs, you have made a serious miscalculation with my friend's involvement. Miss Riddell is on the case now!"

TO BE CONTINUED . . . (to Part 2)

12

SILENCED IN SUDBURY

PART 2

BORDER PATROL

P.C. JAMES
KATHRYN MYKEL

SILENCED IN SUDBURY PART 2

Mini Mystery
#12

Nona

At the station, the detective sat Nona at a cluttered desk. "Have a seat."

Nona scoffed, "As if I have a choice." She wiggled her hands in front of her. "I'm thrilled you opted for cuffing my hands at the front, but do you think you can let one go and cuff me to the chair or something else instead?"

Senior Detective Sheila Shroud, as evidenced by the placard on her desk, looked at her curiously as if to determine whether she could escape while cuffed to a desk chair. She uncuffed one hand and snapped the handcuff to the back of the tubular metal headrest.

The senior detective, who was probably half her age, sat across from Nona and put a manila file folder down on top of a pile of paperwork in front of her.

How does she have a folder on me already? I've only been in their custody for fifteen minutes.

Nona's voice was steady. Though she'd never been handcuffed or detained in her six and a half decades, her resolve in perilous situations was second to none. "And what's this?"

I'm in complete control.

"Please have a look for yourself." The detective nodded towards the file, her bun so tight not a wrinkle showed on her forehead.

Think again, Nona deary, you are definitely not in control of this situation.

"This will shed some light on exactly *why* we have arrested you," Shroud added, in a French-Canadian accent.

Nona took a deep breath and opened the folder. She scanned the documents, flipping through the pages, which were still warm, just off a facsimile machine. "Clever, and what do you think any of this proves?"

"It proves you're not who you claim to be," Shroud replied, as a hint of mischief crossed her brown eyes before she controlled her expression.

"I provided my legal name and my address in the United States. I told you why I was in Canada on vacation, with my good friend. And I alerted you to my super-sleuthing skills. None of which is disproved by these documents."

"How well do you know your friend—*Miss Riddell*?"

"Now you just wait one minute. You leave her out of . . ."

She cut Nona off with a wave of her hand.

"We know she doesn't have anything to do with this. Squeaky clean, that one. But I had to ask." Shroud grinned. "The

United States wants you back immediately, and they have the right to make that happen."

"What about the case of murder in the washroom?"

"We aren't holding you for the murder. You and your friend found yourself in the middle of an undercover operation, and I can assure you, we do not need your assistance on that front."

"So I'm free to go?"

"Free to go back to the US. Yes. We were just holding you for these allegations the Americans have provided as a justification to bring you home."

"You have to know this is ludicrous?"

"Well, yes, I do, but my hands are tied."

Nona shook the cuff. "I believe mine are too."

The detective chuckled.

Well, I guess we've come to an understanding.

"An officer will be here soon to escort you to a cell while we await your transportation."

Okay, maybe not.

"A phone call, at least, before you lock me up in the clinker."

"Of course," Shroud replied, and turned an old-fashioned phone towards Nona.

Pauline

AT THE STATION—AN ugly modern concrete office, in Pauline's opinion—the two officers led Pauline to a cramped office, where stacked files covered every possible surface, including the desk. The driver gave her an *It's going to be okay* look and was led away, presumably to a waiting area.

"Where is my friend?" Pauline demanded.

"Settle down, Miss . . ."

"Miss Pauline Riddell."

"All right, Miss Riddell, may I call you Pauline?"

"No, you may not."

"Okay, Miss Riddell, have it your way. We have detained Ms. Galia, and she will be heading back to the United States tonight."

"Did she explain to you who she suspected the *actual* murder-er was?" Pauline overemphasized "actual" and sounded out "murderer" like she was speaking to a child who had never heard the word before.

"How well do you actually know your *friend*, Miss Riddell?"

At that, Pauline paused for the briefest moment. She eyed the placard on the woman's desk. "Detective Shroud, Gretta and I have been vacationing together . . . and solving crimes . . . for over a decade. Well enough to be certain she is *not* a murderer."

Shroud steepled her hands. "Okay, look, we seem to have started off on the wrong footing here," she said calmly.

"Well, that's obvious. That's exactly what I've been trying to tell you." Pauline sat down in the seat across from the detective.

Shroud put a manila file folder on the table in front of Pauline. Not a slim file with only today's events in it, as thick as a magazine.

How does she have a file on Nona so quickly? We were just minutes behind them? Where did all this evidence come from? In a calm voice, Pauline asked, "And what's this?"

"Please have a look, Miss Riddell. You'll find out just exactly *why* we've detained your *American* friend," Shroud replied.

Pauline hesitated for an imperceptible moment, averted her eyes from the detective, took a deep breath and opened the folder.

"These are American documents," Pauline said, puzzled. "What have these to do with what happened today?"

"Nothing. These documents were sent to us just this afternoon," Detective Shroud replied.

"But why? I can't make heads or tails of any of this."

"It seems your friend isn't all she claims to be." Shroud put her hands on the desk as if to signal the meeting was about to conclude.

"Well, this is all oddly cryptic." Pauline quickly scanned the few words that weren't redacted on the sheet of paper she was holding, before putting the report back in the folder.

I've never seen documents like this before. What has Nona gotten herself into? If I didn't know better, I would say these are fake.

"I would've sensed something if my friend were mixed up in anything nefarious." She pointed to the words *violations, covert, false pretense.*

"Are you sure? Do you live close enough for you to catch her *every move*? Do you go back far enough to understand her *history*?"

"Well, no," Pauline admitted. "She lives in the US, and I live in Toronto, and we met randomly at a cooking class. We do talk regularly on the telephone, and we meet frequently on these trips." She paused to consider, before shaking her head. "No," she said at last, "it's impossible."

"It is possible. Probable even, but there's nothing I can do," Shroud said. "They want her sent back immediately, and those papers give them the right to make that happen."

"Even if I can prove she didn't murder the woman in the restaurant?"

"We aren't holding her for that murder, just for these allegations by the Americans."

"Can I talk to her?"

"No," Detective Shroud said. "Only her lawyer will have access. It's an international case. Not something for private citizens to get involved in."

"There's no connection then, to the dead woman in the washroom?"

"No," Shroud replied. "You and your friend found yourself in the middle of an undercover operation, and I can assure you, we do not need your assistance on that front."

"I have to speak to Nona before you people ship her off to God-knows-what down there in the States," Pauline demanded, but softened and asked, "Can we speak by phone?"

"Here's the number for the chief's office. Give him a call later this afternoon. Maybe he'll accommodate you."

Pauline took the note the woman handed her and said, "As neither I nor our driver entered the coffee shop, or have anything to do with this American charade, I assume we can leave immediately?"

She nodded. "Correct, but give me the information for where you're staying in Sudbury so, if we do need you, we can get in touch." Shroud turned her notepad towards Pauline and placed a pen on top.

Pauline scribbled the details on the paper and then stood. "Good day."

The driver was waiting in the lobby.

"Let's go. Sudbury, and the hotel, as quickly as you can," Pauline said, exiting the station.

Nona

"Liam? What are you doing here?" Nona asked. "And why are you wearing a tie? You never . . ." Nona caught a look in his eye that she didn't like.

"I need to get you transported back to the States, Gretta."

Her friend, and lawyer, had a crease in his brow that rivaled an African elephant. He was clearly worried.

"I figured that out from the looks of those fake documents Detective Shroud showed me. Is that even her real name?"

"I think so," Liam replied, and shrugged.

"You look like someone has died. Tell me what is going on here? And why are you interrupting my vacation?" Nona's words were a barrage of uncertainty. She stood and paced the cell-like room, her concern growing.

"I presumed Pauline was still in the dark, so I came cloaked," Liam replied, with a hint of a grin showing a thin line of his teeth.

"I don't like all this cloak-and-dagger nonsense. Never have." Nona put both hands on her hips and gave him a stern look.

"Well? Isn't she still in the dark?"

Nona sighed, and her hands dropped to her side. "Yes. I just haven't found the right time to tell her about the Society, though I think she's the perfect candidate to join us. I suppose now she'll *have* to be told."

"That choice is entirely yours, Grand Quibah."

Nona groaned. "Honestly, Liam, I can't fathom where you come up with all these theatrics. That's worse than mine."

Liam shot a pointed look at Nona. "If I recall, you came up with that one."

"Well, fine, you might be right. In my defense, a secret society of only women can't go around using 'Poobah,'" Nona scoffed. "An archaic term used by men for centuries!"

"So Quibah is a better option?" He stifled a chuckle, and Nona jutted her chin up in defiance.

"Well, your *male* Lord of Argument has arrived to save the day." His grin turned to a full toothy smile, albeit with false teeth.

At that, Nona couldn't contain her laughter. She cackled so hard she might pee. She crossed her legs and turned away from Liam, pretending to catch her breath from the laughter. "I should be calling you Alfred." Turning back to him, she continued, "All kidding aside, get me out of here already."

Liam's look turned somber. "It's a good thing the Canadians are so hospitable." Liam waved his hand in front of them. The inside of the so-called "jail cell" rivaled a display at the local IKEA, except for the barred door.

"Yes, but I don't like that look at all, Liam. I'm not going to be happy about whatever has brought you here, am I?"

"I'm afraid not. Not at all."

"Then let's get on with it." Nona sat and placed her hands on the edge of the bench seat.

"Not here. We need to get you on the plane first before I fill you in. Your ride, the plane, should be here within the hour. Pauline will be here any minute as well. She insisted on coming back to the station straight away. To ensure your fair treatment, of course."

"That doesn't leave me much time to think of what to say to her." Nona stroked her chin in contemplation. "I think I'll take a page from your book on this one. There will be time to tell her everything later."

She paused and looked at Liam seriously. "Once *I've* been informed as to what's really going on."

"I'll leave you to it," Liam replied, adjusting his tie.

"Hey, what about the dead body in the washroom?"

Liam winked.

"Are you serious, Liam? This wasn't real?" Nona asked. "You duped me?"

"The two officers, Shroud, and the *friend* of the undercover officer. All in on the ruse. I needed to get you to safety."

"Hmm, that's a new one. Finally a vacation where there isn't a murder and you're going to whisk me away." Nona bristled and flashed him a serious look. "Liam, is Pauline in danger?"

"I shouldn't think so, but Shroud will look after her while she's in Sudbury."

"*You shouldn't think so?*" Nona repeated.

"There's no use arguing about *it*, or my methods. Put on a brave face and deal with Pauline, and then we'll be safely on our way home," Liam said, as he disappeared down the hallway. The faint clinking of the cell door caused her to start, and she grabbed the bars of the door.

This is bad, really bad.

Pauline

AT THE HOTEL, Pauline released the driver and gave him a generous tip.

Checking in, she was curt with the hotel staff, impatient to get to the room and call the police chief's office. She snatched her key card off the counter and dragged her bag to the bank of elevators, jamming the up button with her index finger. Staring at her reflection in the mirrored doors of the lift, she took a deep breath.

Get a hold of yourself, Pauline. There must be a logical explanation.

The elevator chimed, and the doors opened. Pauline entered with her suitcase in tow.

Nothing is ever logical when it comes to Nona.

As much as the situation pained her, a quirk of a smile formed on her lips. *That's an understatement.*

Not bothering with anything in her hotel room, she sat on the bedside and dialed the chief's office.

I'm not waiting until this afternoon.

A reluctant secretary put her through after Pauline explained her reason for calling.

"Police Chief Saunders speaking."

"I'm calling to . . ."

"I'm aware of why you are calling, Miss Riddell," he said,

interrupting her. "I was warned."

"Well, can I see her?"

"Once we've finished the paperwork and interview, and if she wants to see you, yes, you can have ten minutes with her."

"When might that be?" Pauline demanded. "I want to see her today before this charade of an arrest goes too far."

"She has a lawyer for that," the police chief responded. "You can visit with your friend."

"Nona and I have solved more crimes than you have had hot dinners. I'm sure, if we can put our heads together, we can sort out whatever has led to this total misunderstanding."

"Ten minutes," he said. "You can see her in about an hour. Come to the station and ask for me personally."

"Then I'm coming there right now," Pauline replied. "I don't trust our governments not to fly her out of the country before letting anyone see her."

"It could be a long wait, but that's your decision."

The moment she hung up the phone, Pauline dialed a new number. This time to a lawyer she knew, Toby Mortimer, who specialized in cross-border cases. The secretary needed to be convinced of the urgency of the situation, but the secretary finally connected Pauline to his cell phone. Pauline explained the case, describing the documents she'd been shown and asking for his advice.

"Based on what you've told me, Miss Riddell," Toby said, "there's little chance of stopping her return to the States. This doesn't present as an ordinary case."

"How can that be?" Pauline said, exasperated. "She's an elderly woman I've been acquainted with for years now. We've solved many cases together. It's not like she's an international terrorist or anything."

"Even misguided people grow old, Miss Riddell. Our countries often get things wrong, but you'll have to prove that down in the United States. In my professional opinion, something is wrong with this picture, and my advice to you is to stay out of it. I suspect a plane is already on its way to collect your friend. You should head home too."

"That's your *professional opinion*? It's not like she's Al Capone," Pauline cried. "This is Nona Galia of Spruce Street in Salem, Massachusetts."

"I'm sorry," Toby said. "I'm afraid there's nothing I can do. You're wasting your time and money trying. I suggest you let your friend get herself out of this pickle."

Pauline slammed down the phone immediately. *Pickle?*

She picked the handset back up to call the front desk for a cab. While she waited for her ride to arrive, she freshened up. Then she made her way down to the lobby where the taxi was waiting for her. The drive from the motel to the prison gave Pauline time to puzzle out what was happening around her friend but not long enough to find an answer. Nothing she imagined made sense.

NOT ONE, but two hours later, and in the presence of a stern police officer, Pauline was allowed into the holding cell where Nona sat apparently unconcerned. The so-called cell was plusher than their hotel room, save for a barred cell door.

She looks less upset than I am.

"I can see you're doing just fine," Pauline said, and crossed her arms.

"I am," Nona said. "It's all worked out."

"So they're setting you free?"

"No. Well, not right away," Nona replied.

"None of the things in the documents they showed me make any sense."

"Nah," Nona said. "It's just a bunch of hogwash. Drummed up to use as *leverage*." Nona air-quoted the word "leverage."

"Leverage for what? The murder of the woman in the washroom? It's not like you were busted for shoplifting at a Wally World."

"Look, Pauline, let the Canadians handle this show. We should leave this one be."

"We always say that," Pauline replied. "And never take our own advice."

"I know, but this time we need to let it go. There is nothing about that charade to investigate," Nona replied. "I've got this." She shook her index finger around in a circle signifying the 'club med jail cell situation'. "I'll be out of circulation for a few weeks, maybe a month tops. I'll contact you, and we can pick up right where we left off."

"'Charade to investigate,' 'out of circulation,' 'pick up right where we left off'. . . Are these coded messages I don't understand?" Pauline questioned, looking up at the ceiling for cameras or listening devices, and not seeing any.

"It'll be fine. I'll explain everything. In time. Enjoy your vacation, everything is paid for. Don't stress."

Pauline blew out a long breath of frustration. "So you're telling me you don't need me to do anything?" She studied Nona carefully for signs of an unspoken message.

"Exactly."

"Time's up, lady," a uniformed officer boomed at Pauline. "Your ride is here," he added, glaring at Nona.

Pauline bent and hugged Nona. "Very well," she muttered, as the officer urged her out. "But you keep me informed. If this doesn't go as you expect, I'm on the outside and can get you help." The officer urged Pauline down the hall. "You hear me, Gretta?"

Nona spoke up. "I will, Pauline. You can be sure of it. Now go before they arrest you too!"

Pauline was escorted outside the building just as quickly. Leaning against the stone facade, she considered her next move. She hadn't trusted Nona's calmness one bit. *Forced, an act, even.*

A cruising taxi caught her eye, and she waved it down.

"Where to, lady?" the driver asked once she was seated.

"Go around the block and stop somewhere where I can watch those gates," Pauline replied, pointing to the wire gates that closed off the parking compound for the station.

The driver flashed her a wary look in the rearview mirror but did as he was instructed. Before he put the vehicle in park, Pauline shouted, "Follow that van!" A black police van drove out of the gates and turned onto the street in front of them.

After a few minutes of pursuit, the driver said, "Looks like we're heading to the airport. Do you still want to follow? It'll be expensive, ma'am."

"Yes, please, continue following."

Less than ten minutes later, the taxi driver pulled up to the airport concourse just as a man in a flashy suit was leading Nona out of the van, surrounded closely by the two uniformed officers from earlier.

Do they really believe she's a flight risk?

They took Nona inside the building, leaving Pauline to ponder, again, her next steps.

Get out and watch your friend leave on a plane, or go back to the hotel, just assuming it will happen?

"How much do I owe you?" she asked.

"Forty dollars even."

She tossed a fifty-dollar bill at him. "Keep the change." Pauline exited the cab and walked into the terminal. She kept her distance while maintaining a visual on Nona, the mystery man, and the officers.

The sun was setting, when a small plane landed and taxied to the terminal. Pauline spied from behind a magazine as the men ushered Nona quickly to the plane. Once inside, the door closed immediately behind them; no other passengers boarded. Pauline stood and walked to the windows. The thundering of the engines revved, and the plane traveled back out to the runway. The red taillights of the plane winked at Pauline as the plane and Nona headed south, disappearing into the dark of the night sky.

Pauline exited the terminal and hailed a new taxi. She gave the driver the name of the hotel and sank into the backseat.

What do I do now?

There's no murder mystery to solve.

Should I finish the vacation or go home?

READ SASSY SENIOR Sleuths on the Trail

READ MORE SASSY SENIOR SLEUTHS MYSTERIES

Read Sassy Senior Sleuths
Read Sassy Senior Sleuths on the Trail

Leave a review!

Thank you for reading our book!
We appreciate your feedback and love to
hear about how you enjoyed it!

Please leave a positive review letting us
know what you thought.

ABOUT THE AUTHOR P.C. JAMES

P.C. James, Author of the Miss Riddell Series

I've always loved mysteries, especially those involving Agatha Christie's Miss Marple. Perhaps because Miss Marple reminded me of my aunts when I was growing up. But Agatha never told us much about Miss Marple's earlier life. While writing my own elderly super-sleuth series, I'm tracing her career from the start. As you'll see, if you follow the Miss Riddell Cozy Mysteries series.

However, this is my Bio, not Miss Riddell's, so here goes with all you need to know about me: After retiring, I became a writer and when I'm not feverishly typing on my laptop, you'll find me running, cycling, walking, and taking wildlife photos wherever and whenever I can.

My cozy mystery series begins in northern England because that was my home growing up and that's also the home of so many great cozy mysteries. Stay with me though because Miss Riddell loves to travel as much as I do and the stories will take us to the many different places around the world I've lived in or visited.

- Facebook: https://www.facebook.com/PCJamesAuthor
- Bookbub: https://www.bookbub.com/authors/p-c-james
- Amazon Author Page: https://www.amazon.com/P.-C.-James/e/B08VTN7Z8Y

- GoodReads Page: https://www.goodreads.com/author/show/20856827.P_C_James
- Amazon Series Page: My Book
- Miss Riddell Newsletter signup: https://landing.mailerlite.com/webforms/landing/x7a9e4

Books on Amazon:
In the Beginning, There Was a Murder
Then There Were ... Two Murders?
The Past Never Dies
A Murder for Christmas
Miss Riddell and the Pet Thefts
Miss Riddell and the Heiress
Miss Riddell's Paranormal Mystery
The Girl in the Gazebo
The Dead of Winter
It's Murder, on a Galapagos Cruise

Cozy Mysteries by Kathryn Mykel & P.C. James:
Senior Sassy Sleuths Series
(Short Stories, Shared Main Characters)
Senior Sassy Sleuths
Senior Sassy Sleuths Return
Senior Sassy Sleuths on the Trail

**1950s Cozy Mysteries by
Kathryn Mykel & P.C. James:**

ABOUT THE AUTHOR KATHRYN MYKEL

Inspired by the laugh-out-loud and fanciful aspects of cozies, Kathryn Mykel aims to write lighthearted, humorous cozies surrounding her passion for the craft of quilting. She is an avid quilter born and raised in a small New England town.

Quilting Cozy Mystery Series:
Sewing Suspicion (Book 1)
Quilting Calamity (Book 2)
Pressing Matters (Book 3)
Mutterly Mistaken
(Holiday Pet Sleuths Series) (Book 3.5)
Threading Trouble (Book 4)
Paw-in-Law
(Holiday Pet Sleuths Series) (Book 4.5)
Stitching Concerns (Book 5)
Purrfect Perpetrator
(Holiday Pet Sleuths Series) (Book 5.5)
Mending Mischief (Book 6)
Doggone Disaster
(Holiday Pet Sleuths Series) (Book 6.5)

Book Set 1
Includes Books (1-3):
Sewing Suspicion, Quilting Calamity & Pressing Matters

Book Set 2
Includes Books (1-5):
Sewing Suspicion, Quilting Calamity, Pressing Matters,
Threading Trouble & Stitching Concerns

For more fun content and new releases, join Kathryn on <u>Patreon</u>, sign up for her <u>newsletter</u>, or join her and her thReaders on Facebook at <u>Author Kathryn Mykel</u> or <u>Books For Quilters.</u>

Bonus Content:
https://sewingsuspicion.mailerpage.com/bonus

Bookbub https://www.bookbub.com/profile/kathryn-mykel
GoodReads Page: https://www.goodreads.com/author/show/
21921434.Kathryn_Mykel

Sweet & wholesome romance by Kathryn LeBlanc:
Quinn (Runaway Brides of the West Series)
Christmas Star Cottage (Holiday Cottage Series)
Sugar Cookie Inn (Christmas at the Inn Series)
Clara's Crusade (Suffrage Spinster Series)

Anthology Series
(Short stories by multiple authors)
A Cauldron of Deceptions (Includes: Kicked the Cauldron)
A Campsite of Culprits
A Vacation of Mischief (Includes: Murder Glazed Over)
Murder Glazed Over
An Aquarium of Deceit (Includes: An Otter Disgrace)
An Otter Digrace
A Bookworm of A Suspect (Includes: A Wisp of Murder)
A Wisp of Murder
A Festival of Forensics (Includes: She Deserved Butter)
She Deserved Butter
A Haunting of Revenge (Includes: Graveyard Shift)
Graveyard Shift
Little Shop of Murders

Printed in Great Britain
by Amazon